# DRIVE TO REDEMPTION

Turning his back on drink and trouble making, Jim Boland returns to Ellsworth sober and ready to start a new life with Rose, his girl. Unfortunately, the marshal who promised Jim a job is dead, and there's something sinister about his replacement. Unexpectedly, Marshal Jake Bradman makes him his deputy. However, will he turn a blind eye to Bradman's suspicious activities, and so remain in Ellsworth — or take his six-shooters, make his own investigations and seriously risk Rose's life?

MIKE DEANE

# DRIVE TO REDEMPTION

*Complete and Unabridged*

**LINFORD**
*Leicester*

First published in Great Britain in 2011 by
Robert Hale Limited
London

First Linford Edition
published 2012
by arrangement with
Robert Hale Limited
London

British Library CIP Data

Deane, Mike, *1980 –*
Drive to redemption.- -
(Linford western library)
1. Western stories.
2. Large type books.
I. Title II. Series
823.9'2–dc23

ISBN 978–1–4448–1344–9

Published by
F. A. Thorpe (Publishing)
Anstey, Leicestershire

Set by Words & Graphics Ltd.
Anstey, Leicestershire
Printed and bound in Great Britain by
T. J. International Ltd., Padstow, Cornwall

This book is printed on acid-free paper

# 1

## Appomattox 1865

He was alone, separated from his unit. His breaths came fast and shallow as he fought to suppress the panic he felt inside. It was growing dark and he could hear the sound of fighting all around. The only trouble was that he didn't know which way his fellow Confederate men were, and which way would lead to a Yankee bullet. He moved slowly, eyes open wide, searching for an ally. Up ahead he could see a small wooden hut, set back from a clearing. He made for it. Maybe he could ride out the skirmish in there. Find his unit when the fighting had finished.

He slunk across the clearing, making for the door of the building. He opened it slowly, his pistol drawn. Gradually he pulled the door back until he could stick his head inside. It was dark, difficult to make anything out. Then the butt of a rifle crashed into the side of his face. He staggered backwards, stunned by the blow, the pain not yet hitting him. He tripped over his leaden feet and collapsed to the ground. He dropped his weapon and as he lay there defenceless, his face feeling as if it was being branded, he stared up at the advancing Yankee soldier. He saw the rifle being levelled at him and figured that this was the end. He thought of his family. Of his wife, Maria, his daughter, Katie, and son, Jim. Thought of how he had left them to look after the farm while he went to war. Went to fight for what he believed in. And how it had led to him waiting to be shot like a stray dog. He wished with all his heart that he had stayed at home, there were plenty of other fellers willing to get shot at, why did he have to go and join them? He said a final silent goodbye to his family, closed his eyes and waited for the end.

Nothing happened. Still he kept his eyes closed, wondering what was taking so long. Still nothing. He dared to look. He was alone. The Yankee's rifle lay in the clearing, just a few feet away. He rose carefully, in case this was some unholy trick that was being played on him. Nobody fired. He picked up the gun, all the while looking around for an attacker. He examined the weapon and found the reason for the Yankee's rapid disappearance. A bullet had jammed in the barrel, rendering the weapon useless. Tom Boland said a silent prayer of thanks, walked off the battlefield and headed for home.

★　★　★

It took him two months to make it back to his homestead and what he found there pained his heart. The buildings were burnt and the stock scattered. He rushed frantically around the ruined buildings, hysterically calling for his loved ones. But there was no reply.

They were nowhere to be seen. He mounted up again and headed for his nearest neighbours, the Mackens. He was greeted by a similar scene. This time he couldn't muster up the energy or the will even to search the homestead or call out in hope. He was exhausted, mentally and physically. He slid off his horse and collapsed on to the ground. He rolled into a ball and cried, the tears and sobs racking his body, the sheer magnitude of what he had lost overwhelming him. The thought of never seeing his family again left him unable even to conceive of how he could go on living.

Then a voice called to him, a timorous, uncertain voice. 'Pa,' it called. 'Is that you? Have you come back for us?'

His head rose, he was unwilling to believe his ears. Was it a voice from beyond the grave that was calling to him? A small figure ran from the ruins of the the barn and headed straight for him. She ran into his arms and he embraced little Katie for all he was worth. She was joined almost immediately by Jim and Maria. They all cried. Cried like they were never going to stop. But this time they were tears of happiness that fell on the scorched ground.

The next few days were taken up with recovering what could be saved from the burning embers and rounding up what was left of the scattered cattle. Tom Boland's homestead was but one of many in the valley that had been destroyed. As he packed up his wagon with his family and what was left of his goods he was joined by nine other families, all in the same situation. The place held too many bad memories for so many of them, so they packed everything into their wagons leaving what used to be home behind. It was the saddest day of their lives, driving up the road leaving everything they had ever known behind except for a couple of cows and a wagon load of supplies.

They were heading west for a new start, a new beginning: ten families, all in the same situation. Nothing to lose but their lives. Day after day they travelled until eventually they reached the Missouri River. Some folks wanted to stop in Kansas and try their luck there but Tom told them that making a living would be difficult on that land. There wasn't enough of it left because those who had come before them had taken all the best land.

There was a big meeting one night of all the folks in the wagon train. Tom was in favour of striking on for Texas; he felt that the plains were there for the taking, good land for whoever wanted it enough. Most of the rest didn't agree, though. They said that there was nothing in Texas except sand and outlaws. Those who didn't want to stay in Kansas wanted to head for Oregon and such places. They talked all night until at last Tom stood and laid his thoughts on the line.

'Well,' he said, 'I see it like this. I've taken my family from their home, from everything they know and love and brought them west, looking for a new start. And that means I sure ain't halting here in Kansas, where a feller can maybe only get enough land for fifty cattle. No man can live like that, at least no man worth his salt! I don't know what the rest of you folks are going to decide to do tonight, but tomorrow my family and I are going to strike out for Texas. I heard what you said about Texas earlier, Hal Burns, but I don't agree with you. There's sand, sure, and outlaws too, and maybe not as much water as most other places. But where there is water there is grass. Long, green, lush grass. Plenty of it. As far as the eye can see in some places. And more important, there are no fences around it. Nobody has claimed it. At least, very few folks have been brave enough to make it there to claim it.'

A voice interrupted him. 'There's a reason for there being so few cattlemen heading for Texas, Tom, and it ain't because they ain't brave. It's because they ain't stupid. They don't want to be scalped by Injuns, or die of thirst, or have to eat their horses. There's no good in Texas, Tom. I mean it. And even if there is some, I ain't planning on risking my family's lives to find it!'

A murmur of agreement ran through the crowd. 'If that's the way you're going to be, John, then that's the way you're going to be,' Tom said. 'I ain't going to try and turn your head. All I'm saying is that I'm heading for Texas and a good tract of land that I can support my family with, and anyone that wants to join me, can.'

John Macken spoke up again. He pleaded with Tom to change his mind. 'It's suicide going on your own. You won't even make it to the Red River,' he said. 'He wouldn't be alone,' answered Dan Mitchell. 'I'd be tagging along as well,' said Mike Connery, 'and me,' said Paul Sullivan. Tom felt as if he was being ripped apart by a mixture of emotions: happiness at the support he was getting as well as a new feeling of responsibility. He felt that he had to get these folks to Texas safely now, and then find land for them too. He hadn't expected to be saddled with all this when he stood up to speak his mind, but that was the way it was. And Tom Boland was a feller who, once he felt something was his duty, made sure he did it properly.

They set off the next morning at the crack of dawn. Four wagons heading for Texas. They said their goodbyes to the others, knowing that they would more than likely never see each other again. There was a tear in more than one eye that morning because, whatever their differences, they had always been neighbours. Always helped each other out whenever there was trouble. And now they would be split up, probably for good.

They rolled out, heading into the unknown. The first few days were quiet travelling, the horses pulling strong, and the cows moseying on alongside the wagons. Then one evening they settled down to camp in a gully. They circled the wagons as best they could: a small circle as there were only four wagons. They built a small fire in the middle of the circle and made sure that the cows were grazing close by. Gradually the sun began to set, one of the most beautiful sunsets that Tom Boland had ever seen. Red, gold and orange streaked across the sky. He sat with his son, Jim, staring at the beautiful show that nature was putting on for them, when Jim grabbed at his arm and clutched urgently at his shirt.

Tom looked at him, curious to know what was spooking his son. Jim just pointed, his finger tracing a path to the top of the ridge overlooking the gully. Tom followed his son's direction and what he saw there chilled him to the bone. Lined along the rim of the rock face was a band of Indians. There must have been about twenty of them, all whooping and hollering. They began to clamber down the hill, their spotted ponies' hoofs driving shale before them. Tom shouted at the others to get ready while Jim just whispered: 'Injuns.'

# 2

Tom grabbed a Winchester from their wagon. He looked over Jim's shoulder at the approaching Indians and thrust the rifle into his son's arms. 'It's time for you to become a man, Jim,' he said. 'You know what you got to do.'

Jim was petrified. His knees were knocking together so hard that he imagined that it sounded like he had a drum between his legs. He had fired the gun before, but only at crows and rabbits, never at another human. The Indians drew closer and Tom rustled up everyone else in the camp who was able to hold a gun. That was, besides Tom and Jim, Mr. and Mrs. Sullivan, the Mitchells and their son John, and the Connerys. Nine guns against twenty. Tom didn't like those odds.

The air was full of dust as the Indians came closer and closer. Tom waited and watched as they neared, Jim beside him trying his best to look brave.

'Wait until they get real close,' Tom said to Jim, 'we don't have many bullets. Make sure each shot is a hit.'

Jim just nodded.

'You'll be fine,' Tom said soothingly. 'You're ready.' Their attackers came within range. Tom yelled: 'Fire!'

Ignoring everything he had ever been taught, Jim closed his eyes as he pulled the trigger. The sound of nine Winchesters filled the air as they unloaded on the Indians. When Jim opened his eyes again there were fewer Indians on horseback and a few more on the ground. Before they could fire again a volley from the Indians forced them to eat some dust as bullets zinged overhead, thudding into the wagons behind them. Straight away Tom was back up again and unloading at them. Again the Indians returned fire and again the convoy responded. The Indians were definitely getting closer but there were also more of them on the ground.

'One more round should finish them off,' Tom shouted over the roar of hot lead. Jim lifted the rifle to his shoulder again and, growing gradually more confident, drew a bead on the first Indian who came into view. He squeezed the trigger. The valley echoed one final time with the sound of guns. The sound seemed to rumble up and down the gully, as if a dam had broken and the gorge was about to be filled with a massive torrent of water.

The smoke cleared slowly, revealing a sight that brought welcome relief to the besieged families. The Indians seemed to have had a bellyful of their lead and had turned to ride off. Some of them pulled on their rope reins so hard that their ponies dropped almost to their haunches as they swung about. One last broadside was sent after them to make sure they didn't think about coming back.

Relief flooded through the veins of the families. They all looked at each other and patted each other on the back. Jim lowered his gun, his arms weak from the strain of the past minutes. He felt as if something had changed. As if he had become a man. He had seen off an Indian raid and was suddenly filled with a feeling of elation. Until, that was, he heard his mother's wailing. Tom ran back to the wagon, chilled to the bone, terror filling his senses. Maria coming out of the wagon, carrying the lifeless form of little Katie, met him.

★ ★ ★

A stray bullet had found its way into the wagon, hitting Jim's sister and killing her instantly. She was only four years old. Tom and Maria collapsed on to the dry ground, crying their hearts out. Jim couldn't move, couldn't understand what had happened. How could something so young, so small, be taken like that? He staggered over to them, his legs moving as if independent from the rest his body. Tom put his arm around his shoulder and they cried and cried. He thought he could never stop crying but eventually Tom got up and pulled Jim up too. 'The Injuns have scattered the cattle. We got to go help the others to round them up, or else they'll get away and we won't be far off joining little Katie,' he said with a cracked voice.

They rounded up the cows, and that evening, after a short service, they buried little Katie, covering her grave with a mound of stones so the buzzards couldn't get her. Jim stared vacantly at the small mound, thinking in his head: 'Why didn't I spot those redskins sooner?'

★ ★ ★

After they had rounded up the cattle and buried Katie they set off again on their journey. No one said anything as they moseyed along. Every day seemed the same, miles and miles of dry, dusty land ahead of them, the sun scorching

15

from above, and their water running lower and lower. For Jim, the nights were even worse than the days. All night long he dreamt of Indians running down the cliff and his mother coming out of the wagon, holding poor Katie. At last, one morning, they travelled through a range of great big brown mesas, and came upon a valley of grassland. It was more a sense of relief rather than a sense of happiness that passed through the group. They had paid a high price to get there, especially the Bolands.

They rode down the bluff on to the land and the cattle started grazing eagerly, thrilled to see some greenery after the long journey. Paul Sullivan, Mike Connery and Dan Mitchell came up to Tom and thanked him heartily. Thanked him for getting them to Texas and to farmland. Tom just stood there listening to them talk before piping up. 'Fellers,' he said, 'you don't have to thank me for nothing. You would have made it here with or without me. Now

I've got something to tell you and I don't want to hear no disagreeing or no fighting. We're moving on from here, me and the family.'

They fell so silent the wind could be heard whistling through the grass. Eventually the others started protesting and pleading with Tom to stay, saying that he'd travelled so far that he should stay where he was, that his family couldn't take much more. Tom would have none of it. He had his own way and his own idea of how to do things and he would not be swayed.

'There ain't enough grass here for four families and I want to strike on further south. You folks are welcome to come with me if ye want, but I think I can see by your faces that ye don't. And that's fine by me. We'll rest here for a few days before moving on.' The tone of his voice discouraged any argument.

Three days later the Bolands set off once more, on the last leg of their journey. After a couple of days' travelling they came upon a broad flat plain. In front of them, as far as the eye could see, was short yellow grass.

Jim said to Tom, 'This ain't going to do; this grass ain't even green.'

But Tom turned to his son and said, 'Son, this'll do just fine. This grass is just perfect for fattening cattle. It's every bit as good as the grass we left behind.'

They settled down on that plain and set their few cattle free to graze, living out of their wagon until they got supplies together. Tom went off to the nearest town and returned a few days later, leading a wagon full of supplies and with a hundred cattle trailing him. They began to build a fine sod house and dug a well. They now had a fine homestead and a herd to go with it. That was the fall of 1865.

# 3

Everything went well during their first years on the land. The cattle thrived on the Texas grass and in the spring of 1868 Tom had such a strong herd that he decided that it was time to drive some of them north to the railheads, where they could be sold to cattle buyers and sent East. Tom and Jim, who was now a young man of eighteen, rounded up fifty head of cattle and joined up with other herds that were being driven north, in order to form one big moving mass of beef, 3,000 head strong. Because they didn't know the trail they let their cattle be taken by a gang of drovers. Tom insisted on riding with them, though, to keep an eye on the cattle and he asked Jim along too. One of Dan Mitchell's sons was to look after the farm with Maria while they were away, having ridden the two days from the valley where they lived.

Just before they rode out Tom turned to Jim. 'Here,' he said, his voice flecked with emotion. He handed Jim two Colt .44s. Jim just looked up at him, unable to speak. Gratitude welled in his throat. Tom then took a leather pouch from around his neck and handed it to Jim. This contained the lead bullet that had jammed the Yankee's gun and saved Tom's life back in Appomattox in 1865. No thanks were necessary as Tom cuffed him gently about the ear and ruffled his hair. Jim strapped the gunbelt on, the weight of the weapons making him feel like a real cowboy. He then hung the pouch around his own neck. He was a man now, and that was for sure.

As well as his new guns Jim had a small blanket and a sombrero for the drive. Even though he wasn't looking forward to sleeping under the stars at night, if his pa was going to do it, then so would he. As they rode away from the homestead Maria gave both Tom and Jim a big hug each.

'Make sure you come back safely,' she said to them. 'I've gotten so used to cooking for ye now that I wouldn't know how to change.'

As they left the homestead behind Jim thought of the fear he had seen in her eyes. Fear that they'd end up like young Katie and never come back again. He vowed to himself that that wasn't going to happen. That he was going to look after himself every step of the way to Baxter Springs and back, and that he wouldn't do anything stupid to put himself in danger. And he didn't. He did something far worse; he put Tom in danger instead.

★　★　★

Everything was new to Jim on the cattle drive. The round-up, the cutting out of the troublesome stock, the remuda following the cattle, and of course settling the cattle down at the start of the drive and getting them used to

21

travelling together each day. The drive began well and Jim settled into the daily routine. The experienced drovers showed him bit by bit each day about how to become a cowboy.

The drive passed quickly for Jim and as they camped for the night near their journey's end he felt like one of the crew. Little did he know what was coming next. He'd thought he'd got on pretty well with the fellers up until then. He'd laughed and joked with Cookie in the chuck wagon, been shown how to lead the herd by Dane on point and so on. There had only been the two surly characters riding flank that he hadn't really got on with. They had treated him like some sort of child, an irritant that they were looking forward to seeing the back of. This annoyed Jim, but Tom told him that some cowboys were like that, and that he should remember them just so that he made sure that he would never become like them. Jim really learned so much on that drive — you could say it set him up for his life in cattle driving, in more ways than one!

It was freezing cold on the range that fateful night, as Jim got ready for the first watch. Even the coffee he was drinking seemed to bring no warmth to his bones. Tom looked across at his son and, seeing him shivering, came over and offered him his own drink. 'You need it more than me, son,' he said. Jim drank the two coffees gratefully, hopped on his horse and headed off for his watch. The last thing he remembered of that night is seeing his pa bedding down beside a small ridge.

★ ★ ★

Jim felt a sharp pain in his ribs. He opened his eyes slowly, the morning sun burning his eyes. Standing over him was one of the drovers; Burton was his name, if Jim remembered rightly. He found it difficult to order his thoughts, his brain felt fuzzy. Burton drew his foot back and kicked Jim solidly in the ribs again. It was then that Jim realized that he was on the ground and the pain in his head started to register. He touched his hand to his forehead and felt the sticky touch of blood.

'Get up, you good for nothing,' Burton was barking. His face was covered in dust and mud and he had a wild look in his eyes. Jim asked him what was wrong, confusion in his voice.

'What's wrong? What's wrong?' Burton shouted back incredulously. Jim could see the look of disbelief in his face but genuinely didn't know what was going on. 'You fell asleep on watch, you thick mule. And do you know what you did then?'

A cold sweat had started to trickle down Jim's back by this stage. He knew he was in serious trouble; falling asleep on watch was a serious misdemeanour. He told Burton that he didn't know what he was talking about.

'You fell off your horse, you clumsy galoot, and when you hit the ground your gun went off and frightened the herd. Caused them to stampede!'

Jim reached for his gun instinctively. It was lying on the ground beside him. He cracked open the chamber and, sure enough, there was a bullet missing. He had never felt worse in his life, at least not until a few moments later. He asked Burton did they lose any cattle?

'You mean did we find any cattle, more like!' the drover answered. Jim could see he was building up to give him another roasting when Billy McConnell came over and told him to ease off. Billy was the trail boss. He whispered something in Burton's ear and pushed him away. Before he went, though, Burton turned around and spat in the dirt. 'That's what happens when you bring kids on a drive,' he said as he walked away.

Jim thanked Billy for helping him out as Billy pulled him up off of the ground. 'I'm real sorry for falling asleep, Billy,' Jim pleaded. 'I don't know how it happened.'

'These things happen,' Billy mumbled.

Jim knew something serious was up with Billy though; something even more serious than the stampede. He wouldn't look Jim in the eye, kept staring at the ground in front of him. 'Jim,' he began, and he put his hand on Jim's shoulder.

Suddenly a cold chill ran through Jim. Shivered him down to his spine. Even though the sun blazed overhead he stood there shivering as though it was the middle of winter. Jim asked him where Tom was, told him that he wanted to see him. Jim knew, just knew, that something was wrong. Billy wouldn't answer him. Jim tried to run back to where he'd left Tom resting the night before but Billy caught him by both shoulders and held him where he stood. This time he did look him in the eye.

'Your pa,' he began again, 'did what a good cowboy does when there is a stampede. He tried to hold the cattle like the rest of us, stop them from breaking into open country. He was at the head of the herd trying to turn them. His horse put his foot in a hole and went down in front of the herd. He didn't stand a chance, Jim; he didn't stand a chance.'

It was lucky that Billy was holding Jim because otherwise he would have hit the ground again. The words went off in his head like dynamite exploding over and over again: *he didn't stand a chance.*

Jim told himself that it wasn't possible, that there must have been a mistake. He asked to see Tom but they wouldn't let him. They told him that they'd buried him already because they didn't want Jim to see the state he was in.

Billy walked away and left Jim alone with his thoughts. He thought of everything his pa had done for them. He'd fought in the war. He'd brought them West and built a whole new home on the best land for miles around when everyone told him he was wrong. How could Jim live up to that? And what about his ma? How could just the two of them farm that land? He looked around him in a daze, occasionally catching the eye of the other cowboys, but they all quickly turned away from him, unwilling to stare at this broken figure. It suddenly struck Jim that he had lost almost all their cattle. How were they going to survive with nearly no cattle and no money? What would Pa say? That was when it really hit him: he had killed his father.

# 4

**Chisholm Trail 1874**

Jim Boland's chestnut mustang snickered as the dust kicked up by the snaking columns of longhorns ahead tickled his nostrils. Jim patted his mount's flank and whispered soothingly to it. 'Easy now, partner, we'll be camping soon for the night. You'll get a break from the dust then.'

*And a welcome break it'll be too, Jim thought.*

It had been a long and uneventful drive thus far. The round-up had taken just under a week, the half-wild cattle being lured into the corral with little trouble. And now six weeks later they were over 400 miles from their starting point in the grassy plains of central Texas. A herd of 3000 head and twenty cowmen were moving towards their camp for the night near the Arkansas River, just fifteen miles from their destination: the notorious cowtown of Ellsworth, Kansas.

Boland was riding at the back of the herd. Even though he had six years experience of driving cattle over the plains, valleys, gulches and dustbowls of the West he still rode as a trail rider, the most uncomfortable place for a cowboy to ride. Although less experienced and less capable riders had more attractive spots at the flank of the herd — and, heck, even the point men couldn't make a steer do what they wanted like Jim could, he wasn't bitter. At least, not on this drive.

He knew what bitterness felt like, tasted like, and he also knew what it did to people, what it turned people into. Bitterness had cost Jim Boland a lot. But bitterness no longer had a hold on this tall, tanned cowboy. His riding prowess was evident to all those who saw him on a horse. Man and animal seemed to move as one; it was as if the horse knew what Boland wanted it to do even before he asked it. But that was Jim Boland, a master horseman and cattle driver, yet a man reduced to making up the numbers on every drive since his first. But the feeling in the pit of his stomach was no longer due to the bubbling of bile caused by his resentment of his less skilled but better treated colleagues. It was due to excitement, expectation. This drive was different for Boland. No longer did he have to work for wages far less than he was worth because he had drunk all his previous money away. This time Jim Boland was on a cattle drive for a reason other than to earn money to drink. There was a light at the end of this particular tunnel.

The sound of muffled coughing interrupted Boland's thoughts. It was young Harry McIntyre. McIntyre had his mouth buried in his glove and his whole body heaved each time he wheezed. Boland waited a moment before, seeing that nobody else had spotted the distressed cowboy, calling out, 'Hey Harry, you all right?'

There was no response from his young companion. He was now coughing so hard that he was having difficulty staying in his saddle. Boland quickly recognized that if Harry lost control of his mount, a loose horse in the middle of a large herd of cattle spelled danger. He shouted to the cowboy some ten yards ahead of him. His name was Burt Jackson, no friend of Boland's, but then not many people were.

'Burt,' he called, 'watch my spot for a second.' Burt jerked his head around and barked something at Boland, but Jim was already on the move. Harry's grey quarter horse, without anyone to rein it in, had cantered forward past the tail-end steers and was suddenly flanked on both sides by cattle. The horse, spooked by the thundering of the animals' hoofs approaching from all sides and also by the razor-sharp horns converging on its soft flanks, whinnied anxiously, a wild look in its eyes.

Boland gently manoeuvred Jesse, his mustang, across the back of the meandering herd, toward the gasping rider.

'Harry, Harry!' Boland called. 'Hold on, Harry,' he shouted more loudly as the younger man began to slide from his saddle. If McIntyre fell now the hoofs of the oncoming cattle would pulverize him. Even worse, the falling rider would startle the cattle, causing a stampede and putting all the cowboys' lives at risk. Boland used his knees to work his horse through what, to many a less accomplished rider, would appear as an impenetrable wall of brown hide. Any sudden movement, any wrong step could bring his ride, or even himself, into contact with a stray horn and then all would be lost.

Boland was now just yards away from McIntyre. The young rider was slumped over his horse's neck; he had completely lost control of his mount. Harry's grey snorted more and more frantically, his neck covered in white sweaty foam. The cattle pushed closer and closer. Horse and cow rubbed together. McIntyre's mount reared, its front legs rising into the air, and a terrified whinny screeched from its mouth. Harry's limp body began to topple sideways. His head lolled to one side and his hat fell to the ground where it was immediately trampled under the hoofs of the cattle.

Only McIntyre's boots catching in his stirrups kept him on his horse now. His mount's front legs landed back on the sandy plain again, the jolt causing McIntyre to begin to slide down the flank of the horse and out of his saddle, towards certain death.

'Harry, hang on,' Boland shouted. He thought he was too late as he saw McIntyre's body being engulfed in a cloud of dry, brown dust.

He kicked Jesse on the final few yards to the ailing cowboy, barely avoiding the pointed horns of the surrounding cattle. Boland stretched out his muscular right arm and caught McIntyre in mid-fall. Years of working the reins of horses had strengthened Boland's limbs and he used all that power right now. With his left arm he gripped the reins of his own horse and with his right he pushed Harry back on to his saddle. He steadied the younger man by putting McIntyre's left arm around his shoulder. Grasping the reins of Harry's horse now as well as his own, Boland started to guide the two steeds out of the teeming throng of cattle. Gently yet forcefully, Boland found a path through the rumbling herd of livestock to safety.

Safe now, away from the bulldozing of horns and hooves, Boland checked McIntyre's condition. The younger man's chest heaved violently as he sat bent over the neck of his horse. Boland shook him by the shoulders, trying to bring him round.

*If it was a sick horse*, he thought, *I'd know what to do.*

'Take it easy, Harry. Deep breaths.' He splashed some water on to his face.

McIntyre's breathing sounded more

regular now until at last the heaving ceased and Harry dragged himself up in his saddle, pushing his weary body back with the aid of his saddle horn. Boland was taken aback momentarily by the state of the young cowboy. Harry's face was a dark-brown hue, not from exposure to the sun, like Boland's, but from the dirt kicked back by the herd. Two streaks ran down his cheeks, starting at his eyes and finishing in little droplets of water at his jawline, giving him the look of a clown who had applied his make-up without the aid of a mirror.

Everything about McIntyre indicated weariness, both physical and mental. It was his first cattle drive and as with all beginners, and Jim of course, he was stationed at the tail of the herd. It was obvious to Boland that the strains of being a drag rider had taken their toll on Harry. The heat, the eternal dust cloud, the need to stay alert and keep the weak, lame or sick cattle up with the rest of the herd, and, of course, the smell, the pungent odour given off by any great movement of animals, which hung in the air all day long had overcome him. These factors were but minor inconveniences for a veteran rider like Boland, but for a young one, like Harry McIntyre, they were huge obstacles on the way to becoming a hardened cattleman.

'Take a drop of this, Harry; make you feel better.' Boland handed McIntyre his canteen. Harry lifted it to his lips, threw back his head and drank gladly.

'Thanks, Jim, I'm afraid I ran out of water a couple of hours ago; been too ashamed to ask anyone for a drink since.'

'Don't worry about it, Harry. I figured you'd finished your water all right, no liquid has touched those dusty lips of yours for quite a while, I reckon!'

'Jeez, Jim, you sure do notice the small things. I was dying with the thirst from a long way back; then the dust started getting in my eyes and I used the water to wash it out!' McIntyre hung his head. 'I don't know, Jim, it just seemed like everything I done made things worse,' he muttered, his voice almost a whisper.

'Look, Harry, there's no point making yourself feel any worse than you already do, so all I'm going to say is it's all right to make a mistake. Everyone makes mistakes, just don't make the same mistake twice, y'hear!' Boland even surprised himself with this piece of positive advice; maybe this drive really was different!

Harry looked up at the jagged, bronzed face of the man who had just saved his life and thought that even though the two riders weren't much apart in age, they were years apart in terms of wisdom and experience. Boland pushed away Harry's outstretched hand as he tried to return the canteen.

'Hold on to it until we camp, and remember, it's for drinking, not washing your face.' Harry nodded sheepishly.

'Hey, Boland, get back over here and

watch your damn cattle!' a gruff voice called from somewhere over the other side of the herd. 'This ain't no time for talking; you've got work to do.' Harry, feeling that he should repay his saviour somehow, opened his mouth to defend Jim but Boland, guessing this, raised his gloved hand to McIntyre.

'Forget it, Harry, these clowns don't deserve to be given an explanation.'

'But I just want to repay you someway, Jim, it's the least I can do.'

'Don't worry about it, Harry. I know that if you saw me in trouble you'd come and help me out just like I helped you today. That's good enough for me.' Jim tipped his hat before swinging Jesse around and picking his way through the steers and back to his station at the rear of the herd. Burt Jackson was waiting for him with an impatient scowl on his face.

'Where the hell were you?' asked Jackson.

'Just checking on a friend. You got a problem with that?'

'I ain't paid to ride around in this dust and muck all day long — you are!' Jackson roared, poking a finger into Boland's chest. 'Now stay here and don't go wandering off again or you just mightn't make it to collect your pay!'

He jerked the reins of his gleaming black stallion, and turned and rode away from Boland, back towards his post at the middle of the column, the hoofs of his horse adding to the swirling cloud of grime. Boland spat some dust out of his mouth, momentarily regretting having given his canteen to McIntyre.

'Take it easy, Jim. Calm down,' he murmured to himself. This time the growing feeling of anger and resentment was easier to quell. All he had to do was to think of the reason why he was on this drive, the reason he had worked so hard and drunk so little for the last year.

*No need to get angry and mess things up. Just remember, this is your last night ever on a cattle drive, Jim, your last night ever.*

This thought lifted a weight from Boland's shoulders and, as he straightened in his saddle, a thin smile played on his lips. As he looked ahead the cloud of dust didn't seem so thick, and each step onward brought him closer to the end of the trail. Closer to a new life and, hopefully, redemption.

# 5

As the column approached the slow moving mass of the Arkansas River the trail boss, a swarthy character called Jack Dever, decided that the herd should be bedded down for the night. The cowboys spread out around the cattle, directing them into a slow-moving circle. Round and round went the cattle until they came to a standstill, trapped in their ever-tightening corkscrew before settling to graze peacefully on the range grass beneath them. As soon as the cattle were settled down for the night Jim urged Jesse away from the herd. He dismounted and walked the last few feet to the edge of the overhang on which they had camped for the night. Boland was silent as he stared at the sight in the middle distance: the streets with their wooden saloons and dwellings, smoke rising from their chimneys.

The town of Ellsworth. *Almost there, Jim. Just one more night, then . . . .*

Soon, the night watch was assigned and those fortunate enough to avoid this settled down to eat and then grab some sleep. Jim sat alone, apart from the rest of the riders. He chewed slowly on his salt pork and beans, staring at the lights of night-time Ellsworth.

*Just one more night . . . .*

The sound of soft footfalls breaking the dry range-grass alarmed Boland. He lay stock-still, ears strained, searching for any clue as to who or what might be approaching. Jackson's words echoed in his head: *You just mightn't make it to collect your pay.* Closer and closer the footsteps came, padding gently towards him. Boland slowly but smoothly slipped his hands to his hips and drew out his twin Colt .44s by their dull white handles. He rose gradually until he was on his haunches and made his way bit by bit towards where he thought the prowler was coming from.

*If I could just get around behind*

*him, I could take him by surprise.* Boland could now make out the silhouette of a figure against the moonlit sky. He couldn't tell who the figure was, however, as he was bent slightly, obviously trying to make as little noise as possible. Strange, thought Boland, he doesn't have his gun drawn. Boland crouched down behind a large cow, which, oblivious to the drama unfolding so close at hand, was chewing the range grass peacefully.

*Don't give me away now, pet, just keep on filling your belly.*

Boland was just feet away from the creeping form now. Suddenly he got to his feet and took two quick steps towards his prey. As his foot touched the dry ground for the second time it shattered a twig, the sound resonating like a pistol-shot around the camp. Boland's quarry spun around to see what had caused the sound, his hands flashing to his holsters. But Boland was too fast for him. Before a gun could be drawn Jim was upon him, his Colt rammed up into the underside of his stalker's chin.

'I know it's a mighty fine night for taking a walk, partner.' The words hissed from between his gritted teeth, his skin was pulled taut on his face. 'But you'd better start doing some explaining as to why you were creeping up on me like that. And talk fast, because I feel like I got a mighty twitchy finger tonight!'

'J-Jim, i-it's me. Harry. Harry McIntyre. Remember, y-you saved my life today?' came the trembling voice from the other end of his gun. Boland was shocked into silence for a moment, but only for a moment.

'Harry, what in tarnation were you doing creeping up on me like that?'

'I-I was just . . . Would you mind taking that shooter out of my gullet, Jim? I'd find it much easier to talk that way.'

'Oh. Sure, Harry. Sorry,' Boland muttered, taking down his piece but not holstering it.

'I was just coming to say thanks for today. I was just creeping along in case you were sleeping. I didn't want to wake you, Jim, that's all. If you hadn't seen what was happening today, I don't know what might have happened to me. I sure don't think any of those other fellers would have done anything. I think they'd have gambled on which steer I'd have fallen under instead of trying to save me!' Harry's words came fast; he wished he had left Jim alone now.

Boland chuckled softly. 'I don't know about that, Harry, but thanks anyway. Like I said today, I hope you'd do the same for me.'

'Definitely, Jim, without a shadow of a doubt.' Harry drew a deep sigh of relief as Boland put his gun back in his holster. A low rumbling laugh escaped through Boland's lips.

'Sorry for being so rough with you, Harry, what with sticking my gun in your throat and all. Afraid I've learned not to trust anyone else much, other than old Jesse over there the last few years,' Boland said, nodding to his horse. McIntyre rubbed his neck vigorously, clearly appreciating that it was still attached to the rest of his body. 'I'm just glad that you don't shoot first and then ask questions later, Jim.'

Once again Boland laughed drily. 'Yeah, you sure struck lucky twice today Harry!'

'I got something to ask you, Jim,' said Harry. Boland pushed his hat back from his head, an inquisitive look on his face. He nodded to Harry to continue. Harry took off his hat and held it in his right hand. He looked down at the dusty ground as he began to speak.

'Well, Jim, it's like this. I don't know anything except how to work with cattle. Ma and Pop didn't believe in schooling. Rounding up a herd of cattle was an education in itself, they used to say. What I'm trying to say is that I'd like to be a darn good cattleman, a good cowboy. But today showed me that I have a lot to learn, and it also showed me that you'd be the perfect feller to teach me. What you don't know about cow-herding ain't worth knowing. So if it's all right with you, I'd like to ride with you. Be your partner?'

Silence filled the air, broken only by the sounds of the animals settling themselves for the night.

'Well, Harry,' Jim began, 'you sure said some nice things, there. But I don't think they're necessarily true. There are a lot better people to learn from than me. Heck, I'm only a drag rider like yourself! You should be asking the fellers riding at the head of the herd for help, not me. There ain't much to learn from me. I'm afraid, Harry. I get covered in the same dust as you do every day!'

Then Boland's voice dropped to barely above a whisper as he went on: 'Don't you wonder why I'm still riding drag even though I've been on more drives than any man I ride with? I can't be much good then, can I, Harry? I know that the fellers talk about me too,

48

and I know that you listen — whether you want to or not. So I think you'd be better off staying away from me, Harry. I'm a bad influence. I bring bad luck wherever I go. I'm an outcast. And if you're seen with me you'll be an outcast too. Go back to the campfire, Harry, do your work on the range, on the drive. Stay at it long enough and you'll be riding point someday, at least that's the idea.' Boland's voice had an edge to it, a hint of bitterness was creeping into his words. He took off his hat and ruffled his hair. 'Well, that's the size of it, Harry, as far as I can see. Go on back to the other fellers before they start talking about you behind your back too.'

He liked McIntyre. Thought he was a good kid. Make a good cowboy one day, if he worked hard. But he knew that for Harry to ride with him regularly would lead to him being branded an outsider, a loner and a troublemaker. And that would spell the end of any hopes Harry had of becoming a renowned cattle driver. Boland turned his back on McIntyre and began to walk back to his blanket and what was left of his cold supper.

Harry paused for a moment before speaking again. He was choosing his next words carefully. 'Well, I figured you for many things, Boland, but I never figured you for a yellow-bellied quitter!'

# 6

Boland stopped in his tracks.

'I know I didn't hear you call me yellow, McIntyre.' His voice was as cold as gunmetal and carried as much menace.

'That's another thing you got wrong then, Boland, because what I actually called you was a yellow-bellied quitter!'

Boland spun on his heel, grinding the dust underneath it as he turned. He covered the ground between himself and McIntyre in a matter of seconds, his spurs jingling as he moved. Boland poked a finger into McIntyre's chest forcefully, obliging him to take a step back.

'Let me tell you something. I ain't no yellow-belly, and I certainly ain't no quitter, so it seems to me that you're the one who's got it wrong!'

'Really?' Harry had to fight hard to

maintain his composure.

'Yes, really. While you were still sitting on your ma's apron I was fighting off Injuns on the plain.'

McIntyre came back, giving as good as he'd got. 'Well, I ain't ever heard tell of anything you've done that makes me think that you're nothing more than a god-forsaken drunkard!'

'Let me tell you something, kid!' Boland was furious now, his eyes burning. Small specks of foam formed at the corner of his mouth as he spat the words at McIntyre. 'I've done things in my life that you couldn't even think of. You know that I killed my father, that's followed me always, and will to my grave. Until you have to live with something like that maybe you and all the other jiggers shouldn't be so quick to judge me. I did drink too much, to help forget the pain. But that's all over now.'

Harry had no ready answer this time. 'You can't keep beating yourself up over your pa's death, Jim, you just can't. It was an accident. You made a mistake but you just paid a higher price than most, that's all,' he muttered.

'Always seems to be the case,' Boland sneered. 'But, believe it or not, Harry McIntyre, I agree with you.' There was a ferocity in Jim's voice that took Harry aback. 'I have been beating myself up about it for long enough. I've done my time drinking in saloons so as to forget it ever happened. Had my fallings out with fellers who cussed me and called me a murderer. And do you know what, Harry?'

'What?' asked Harry.

'I've had enough. I'm on my last cattle drive. I've been riding drag on cattle drives for the last six years solid. I've ridden more times up and down this trail than you've had hot dinners, Harry boy, and I've never been so much as given a smell of riding point, or even swing or flank. And d'you know why?' Harry shook his head. 'Because everywhere I go I'm known as the jigger who killed his father and lost his family's herd by falling asleep on watch. But no more.'

A grim smile spread across Boland's mouth. He turned away from McIntyre and cast his hand toward the dim glow that the lights of Ellsworth cast on to the dark horizon.

'One year ago, Harry,' Boland's voice was low now, and softer. He was almost unrecognizable from the man who had spoken so violently a few minutes before. 'One year ago this week, I rode into that town with a herd, just as I had ridden into I don't know how many towns, and I found something there that I had never known even existed. Or if I did once know, had long forgotten about.'

He turned to Harry and looked him straight in the eye. 'And tomorrow, Harry, I'm going to ride in there again, except this time I plan on staying.'

After Harry had left to go back to his pitch Jim once again turned his eyes towards the dull light tinting the horizon. He felt a great sense of longing, a sense of expectancy filling him. He went back to his berth by the ridge and tried to catch some shut-eye before the sun rose, but something kept him awake all night. It wasn't the hard ground or the swirling dust or the coarse scrub. It was something he hadn't experienced in a long, long time. It was that sense of longing, that sense of expectancy that kept him awake that night. He was anticipating the end of his last ever cattle drive, and what awaited him at the end of it.

The cattle drovers were greeted by a bright red sun the next morning, the sky filled with streaks of orange. Even though Jim set off on another day in the saddle without having had any sleep the night before he didn't feel in the least bit tired.

Harry McIntyre looked sideways at Jim as he sat upright on Jesse, his Winchester protruding from his saddle scabbard. He'd heard all the stories about Jim Boland. About how it was his fault his father got killed on that drive.

About how, when Jim had made it back home to the ranch and told his mother that another member of her family was dead, it seemed that she had lost the will to live. He had heard also that young Jim had been so bitter about the incident that he took to drinking soon after and pretty much left his mother to run the ranch by herself. Soon, between losing the cattle the year before and their poor management, they lost their farm and their livelihood.

Harry had also been told that Jim's mother had headed back East after that; there was nothing to hold her in Texas except maybe a drunkard son. Jim, however, decided to stick it out where he was. Some had said that his mother had disowned him, that she wasn't able to look at his face as it reminded her of her husband and the fact that her son had killed him.

Soon after his mother had left Jim's drinking got even worse. He took odd jobs on various ranches so he could make enough money to keep him in liquor. Every spring he began his work on the cattle trails, drinking his way up to Kansas and back down again. They said he'd visited every saloon between the Red River and Kansas, not to mention all the watering holes in North Texas. Many of the jobs he got were given out of sympathy for a feller down on his luck but Boland's constant drinking and troublemaking made sure that those jobs dried up faster than bones in the desert.

Jim drank all his money away. Drinking quickly turned to talking, talking turned to arguing when people told him that he was only half the man his father was, and arguing quickly turned to fighting. The handles on Jim's .44s were dulled with being constantly reached for. He never got the chance to use them in a fight though. Respect for his father caused people to stop him just as he was about to cause himself some serious damage. Jim Boland had come mighty close many times to being involved in a shoot-out with a far more experienced gunman than he, but always the situation had been defused.

But patience only lasts for so long before it runs thin and Jim was running out of people to do his talking for him. When he had left on the drive the year before, nobody would have been surprised if he took on the wrong guy and didn't make it back. But make it back he did.

★ ★ ★

Liquor sure had a hold of Jim, all right, thought Harry, if half of what I've heard is true. But the image of a troublesome drunk wasn't the Jim Boland that Harry McIntyre knew. Or at least thought he knew. Harry couldn't reconcile Jim's actions of the previous day, when he had saved his life, with the idea of the bar-room brawler that he had been led to believe Jim to be. Harry refused to believe that Jim Boland, the man who moved with the grace and poise of a master horseman and cattle herder, could possibly alienate himself from so many people, could be so abrasive as to be thought of as a social outcast.

But then he cast his mind back to the night before and his discussion with Jim. He thought of how he had nearly got his head shot off just for being concerned so as not to disturb him. He thought of how his request to ride with Jim was turned down in no uncertain terms. He remembered the tightening of Jim's lips at times during the conversation and the look of frustration, of repressed bitterness at his lot in life creeping into his eyes. This was in stark contrast, Harry reflected, to the air of lightness, of something close to happiness that came over Jim as he spoke of his arriving in Ellsworth. Though what could give a man anything more than temporary peace and a bad hangover in that town, judging by the tales he'd been told, fooled Harry.

He shook his head and chuckled quietly to himself. He sure is a mystery, he thought. I'm darned if I know what to make of him! One thing's for sure, if this really is his last drive then the cattle trade is going to lose one fine cowboy!

Harry inhaled sharply through his front teeth, the air causing a whistling sound as it passed into his mouth. Must be something special to cause him to give up all he knows, no matter what he thinks or says about it. Takes a lot for a cowboy to leave the cattle trail for good. Especially when it's been his life for so long. A smile passed over Harry's face quickly and a mischievous light sparkled in his eyes. I think I might just ride into Ellsworth and find out what's so great it's taking Jim away from us, he mused. Might be able to get some of it myself!

With that, the smile returned to Harry's face, except that this time it stayed there in the form of a broad grin. He looked forward to the completion of the drive even more now, so that he could follow Jim into Ellsworth and try to unearth a clue to help solve the mystery that was Jim Boland.

# 7

At last, the herd reached the outskirts of Ellsworth. The sun was low in the sky and the cool night air was causing a few of the cowboys to raise their collars to keep in whatever warmth they could. The cattle were safely corralled for the night, ready to be loaded on to the rail cars the next morning. One by one the cowboys received their payoff gleefully and rode off into town, whooping and hollering as they went. Jim could tell that some had reached town already by the sound of pistols being shot into the night air. Eventually it came to Jim's turn to be paid.

Trail boss Jack Dever handed him his wages. 'Jim,' Dever began, 'am I right in hearing that it's your last drive?' Dever was a veteran of several drives and had earned a reputation of being a hard but fair boss. He was also known for his straight talking. Jim glanced at Dever, taking in his bronzed, weather-beaten face. Dever's forehead was creased, causing the lines that ran across it to look like furrows in a sandy field.

'You hear right, Jack. I'm making a new start.'

'Not many fellers would choose this dump for making a new beginning, Jim.'

'Afraid beggars can't be choosers.'

A wry chuckle escaped from Dever's mouth.

'You know, sometimes you remind me of your father, Boland. I really do hope that the change will help you. I can see you've given up the liquor and you've done a top-class job on this drive with me. But I'll be frank, Jim. I don't know if you're strong enough to make it. I've seen fellers give up drinking before and go back to it even harder. I just hope you're not one of those fellers. I hope you prove me wrong and make yourself a success here. It ain't going to be easy, mind, but there must be something drawing you to this place.' Dever paused before continuing: 'I knew your father, Jim. Not very well, but well enough to know what a good man he was. Now, I don't think that a man as good as him can have a son and not have some of his qualities rub off on that son. Deep down I think you're a good man too, Jim. Too damn good to lose your life to drink and to spend it feeling sorry for yourself because fellers say you killed your father. Forget about it, Jim. Whether it was your fault or not doesn't matter. He's dead.

'Now, go and start again like you said. Give yourself a second chance — and promise me one thing, Jim Boland, promise me that you'll take it because there's a lot of good in you, don't be afraid to let people know that!' Without another word Dever rowelled his horse and rode away, leaving a stunned Jim Boland staring after him.

With Dever's words still ringing in his ears, Jim rode on towards Ellsworth.

As he moseyed into town he was confronted by the usual sounds of drunk cowboys raucously enjoying themselves. Jim looked around at the town he hadn't seen for a year. It was clear that Ellsworth was developing into a fully fledged cattle town. Where there had been open spaces and dry, arid land the year before, there now stood saloons and hotels — sure signs that the cattle trade had brought money to the area.

The population of Ellsworth was now about 1,000 souls and the chief business was the trafficking in cattle and trade with the cattlemen. The main street ran along both sides of the railroad, making an exceedingly wide street, or two streets, called North Main and South Main. The business section was about three blocks long. The store buildings, mostly one- and two-storey frame structures with porches on the front, lined the outer side of the street and faced the railroad. Here and there more pretentious structures of brick had been erected. Board sidewalks were generally in use except for a stretch of sidewalk twelve feet wide of magnesia limestone in front of Larkin's Hotel.

It was said that no other town, not even Kansas City, had a sidewalk equal to it. Most of the business places provided benches or seats for loafers under the wooden awnings. There were hitching posts in front of the stores to which farmers' teams or cow ponies were tied most of the time, day and night.

There were many businesses in the town, including hotels, clothing stores, banks, drugstores, hardware and supply stores and of course the general store which sold everything from high-grade groceries to wines and liquors. For medicinal purposes, of course. The railroad station was situated directly across from this store.

The courthouse and jail were on the north side of the railroad tracks. The local paper described the jail as 'the most comfortable place in town,' but also warned its readers that 'too many should not crowd into the building at once.' Nearby was the lumberyard and further on was the Grand Central Hotel. This building was constructed of a good quality red brick and was said to be the finest and costliest house west of the Missouri, excepting in Topeka.

The stockyards were situated up the railroad track in the west part of town; they were constructed of unpainted lumber and covered several acres of ground. The yard had seven chutes from which 200 cars of cattle a day could be loaded. These yards were the largest in the state. The cattle traffic brought to Ellsworth hundreds of drovers, buyers and speculators, and the rough element, which moved from town to town with the shifts of the trade, congregated there. Ellsworth was certainly not the most moral town in the world and during the cattle season, which only lasted during the summer and fall, in the streets could be seen men from every state, and almost every nation. The tall, long-haired Texas herder, with his heavy jingling spurs and pair of six-shooters; Mexicans; gamblers from all parts of the country, looking for unsuspecting prey; the honest emigrant in search of a homestead in the great free West; the keen stock buyers; the wealthy Texas drovers; dead-beats; pickpockets; horse thieves and so on. It was into this great melting-pot that Jim rode.

As Jim was taking in all these changes he didn't notice the large crowd gathered ahead of him and would have ridden into it if Jesse hadn't flinched at a sudden concerted cheer that rose up from the gathering. As the crowd were blocking the whole road Jim decided to dismount and see what was holding the interest of so many cowboys when they could be in saloons, drinking. He slid off Jesse's back and hitched him to a nearby railing.

'Now don't you go off wandering into no saloons, partner, I can barely look out for myself without having to

67

watch out for you too!' he joked.

Jim attached himself to the back of the crowd. 'What's going on?' he asked of the nearest person.

'It's the new marshal, some fellers say. They say he's laying down the law tonight but I can't hear because some people won't shut up!' this person snarled, glaring at Jim. Boland instinctively stiffened. A new marshal; this was not good news. Jim had got to know the previous marshal last year, and had even secured a promise from him to help Jim find work when he returned. Already, it seemed to Jim, things weren't going as planned. He decided to find out for himself who was at the centre of all this commotion and pushed his way into the middle of the congregation.

'Citizens of Ellsworth!'

Jim could now hear the voice clearly but could not make out the speaker just yet.

'And, of course, all you good men of cattle.' A loud cheer went up amongst the drunken crowd. 'I'm here to tell you what my policies as the new marshal of this town are.' The crowd hushed abruptly.

'Remember Tom Smith of Abilene, who could fight outlaws with his bare hands, and banned guns from that town?' A murmur of discontent flowed around the mass of people.

'I hope he isn't going to try and be as tight as Tom Smith. Nobody can enjoy himself with that kind of feller around,' mumbled the man next to Jim.

Jim allowed himself a wry smile at the man's words. He realized that that would just be the kind of thing he would have said a year ago, before he had learnt the value of law and order.

'What would you rather then?' Jim began. 'Drunken fellers like yourself walking round with guns in their pockets, ready to shoot you if they didn't like the look on your face?' His companion was taken aback by Jim's interrogation. His bushy whiskers twitched nervously as he tried to think of an answer. He scratched his stubbled chin frantically as if trying to warm his mouth up in order to reply.

'W-well,' he began.

'Well, I ain't going to be like Tom Smith of Abilene.' The marshal had begun again. Once more a loud roar rose from the throng, none shouting louder than the feller Jim had just been talking to. 'Where's Tom Smith now?' the marshal shouted. 'Six feet underground!' Once more a rowdy cheer surrounded Jim.

'You fellers can keep your six-shooters, but let me tell you one thing.' The tone of the new marshal's voice caused the horde to hush. 'If any of you jiggers think you're going to shoot up my town, you got another thing coming. I don't wear these fellers for decoration.' Jim presumed he was holding up his guns. 'I'm well able to use them if needs be but I sure wouldn't want to be on the receiving end of my shooting if I was you! Anyway, fellers, go and enjoy yourselves tonight. And just remember, there's a new lawman in town, and his name's Jake Bradman!'

The night sky was quickly filled by hats flung by cowboys as soon as Bradman had finished his impressive address.

*I've got to get myself a look at this jigger, he sounds more like a showman than a lawman to me,* Jim thought.

Many gruff voices cursed him as Jim banged shoulders as he fought his way through the crowd. Eventually he came close to where the lawman had just given his speech. Gradually, the crowd thinned in front of Jim until there was just one figure standing there. Jim stepped instinctively back into the shadow of a saloon awning. There was something about this man that did not seem right. He wasn't sure what it was but he thought it better to stay out of sight rather than let his presence be known.

Bradman cut an impressive figure. Looking at him from the side, Jim

71

could see that his dark shirt contained a muscular torso. Both his shoulders and his thick arms indicated that he wouldn't be a person to get in a fist-fight with. Slung around his waist were two six-shooters, sitting snugly in their holsters. Jim figured that Bradman must have arrived in Ellsworth only recently, because he still wore a pair of black-leather batwing chaps over his trousers. The toes of black boots were just visible outside the chaps.

Bradman pulled his hat a little lower over his face as he began to roll a cigarette. He turned toward where Boland was standing, causing Jim to push back even deeper into the shadows. Jim wondered for a second whether he had been seen but as the marshal continued to roll his cigarette he guessed that he hadn't. When he had finished preparing his smoke, Bradman drew it to his lips and lit a match off the heel of his boot. The wooden stick flared momentarily before Bradman's face and flickered before settling into a steady flame. That brief flash of light was enough to cause Jim to take a sharp intake of breath, surely audible to Bradman. What had caused Jim to react like that was that he got a look at the face of Jake Bradman in that instant the match glowed its brightest, and what he had seen shocked him. For, even though his body appeared to be that of a strong and fit man, one side of his face bore a terrible scar — a legacy of a bygone battle, Jim presumed. The scar began at the jawline on the right side of his face and continued to just below his eye. Even though the disfigurement stopped there, the person or persons who had caused it obviously had not, for Jake Bradman wore a large black eyepatch over where his right eye should have been.

# 8

Jim recovered his composure quickly. Bradman was now looking directly towards him. Jim was almost holding his breath now, hoping that Bradman hadn't spotted him. Bradman continued staring however, and kept smoking his cigarette. He took one step towards the awning. Jim now pushed himself back as far as he could. He felt the touch of the wooden wall behind him and now knew that he could move no further. All he could hope for was that Bradman didn't come any closer to investigate. The marshal took another step towards Jim, and then another. He stepped into a shadow caused by the saloon's awning.

All Jim could see coming towards him was the glowing tip of Bradman's cigarette, his dark clothes invisible in the shadow. Why was he hiding from this man? What was it that was causing him to be holding his breath, trying to disappear into the darkness in order not to be found out? He tried to rationalize the matter to himself. This was the marshal! Why was he hiding from the marshal? He'd done nothing wrong. Why not just stroll out and meet him? But deep down Jim knew this wasn't going to happen. He knew that the only way that he would be talking to the marshal any time soon would be if Bradman found him under the awning. Jim certainly wasn't going to give himself up to this man whom he distrusted for some unknown reason.

Bradman was just feet away now; his cigarette almost finished. Abruptly, he stopped, took the cigarette from his mouth, threw it to the ground and crushed it. He gave one last long stare towards where Jim was cowering and spat. He spun on his heel and walked away, not looking back. Jim dared not move until Bradman had disappeared down the street, his batwing chaps rubbing together as he walked. He exhaled gratefully, blowing out his cheeks. A great feeling of relief descended upon him. He certainly hadn't expected to spend his first night back in Ellsworth hiding from the law!

As he emerged from beneath the awning he scanned the street in both directions, making sure that the coast was clear, before heading back to Jesse. He grabbed Jesse's reins, unhitched him from the rail and led him away from the saloon. 'Time to get where we're going, partner, and stop lurking around in shadows. That's just for jiggers.' He shook his head, 'I've got to stop talking to my horse,' he said ruefully.

Jim allowed himself a smile. Ellsworth seemed to have grown in the last year. Now the saloons, hotels and whorehouses covered even more ground than before. Ellsworth was the cowboy's idea of heaven, especially after a long cattle drive surrounded only by other men. It allowed easy access to liquor, gambling and, most important, women. Jim and Jesse passed by saloons, from which customers were falling drunkenly out through their doors. This was a scene repeated all the way down the street. Every establishment was packed to the rafters, full of cowboys determined to drink themselves into having a good time and not caring whom they upset while they did it. Jim guided Jesse to a hitching rail outside a saloon called the Southern Belle, obviously named with attracting the Texans in mind.

Jim patted Jesse reassuringly as he hitched him to the rail outside the saloon. He took a deep breath to settle himself before pushing through the swing doors and into the saloon. Inside, bedlam reigned. In one corner sat suited card-sharps, drinking their liquor studiously and fleecing those cowboys who drank their alcohol with a little more abandon. In another corner a piano was being played, the tune barely audible above the patrons' attempts to sing. Jim took all this in with one wide glance around the room and made his way to the counter.

What Jim hadn't noticed as he entered the bar, however, was that a figure had followed him in. The stranger had his hat pulled down over his eyes and he too scanned the room, just as Boland had. Instead of following him to the counter, though, he chose to lean against the right-hand wall, some ten feet behind Boland, and so kept the whole bar within his field of vision. A young lady came over to this man, tray in hand.

'What can I get you?' she asked.

He looked up into her face and struggled to find words to answer her. He was shocked by her intense beauty. Dark-red curls flowed down to her shoulder, framing a perfectly formed face. Strong cheekbones accentuated her face below deep-blue eyes. Her lightly reddened lips were parted slightly as she waited for his reply.

'A whiskey'll do just fine,' he mumbled at last.

'On the way.'

The stranger couldn't keep his eyes off her as she walked away. He was entranced by the swaying of her body as she made her way to the bar.

'She's something else, ain't she?' asked the patron next to him, clearly as captivated as he was.

'She certainly is.'

She passed around the side of the counter and went to the row of bottles stacked on shelves behind the bar. Suddenly, a voice called to her. 'Hey, pretty lady, what say you get me a drink?' The stranger's attention was immediately aroused: the voice was Jim Boland's.

# 9

'Just wait one minute,' the girl began as she turned to look at who was calling her. She stopped mid-sentence as Jim raised his hat and looked straight at her. A look of shock crossed her face, quickly followed by one of extreme joy.

'Jim!' she cried, and rushed to him, flinging her arms around his neck.

'So that's what's brought Jim Boland to Ellsworth,' the stranger leaning against the wall muttered to himself.

'I wasn't sure you were ever going to come, you should have been here weeks ago!'

'I know, Rose, it sure was a slow drive for my last one!'

'I thought something had happened. I hadn't heard from you in a while.'

'Afraid mail service ain't so good out on the range,' Jim joked.

They spoke quickly and excitedly,

struggling to keep their emotions in check.

'What can I get you?' asked Rose, her demeanour changing suddenly. She appeared more businesslike all of a sudden.

Boland was worried for a second, thinking he had done or said something wrong. A quick look to his left allayed such fears however. A portly, older man had emerged from a door behind the bar that led to the living quarters in the building. Jim recognised this bald, sweating man as Rose's father, Cole. And judging by her reaction she didn't think he'd be too impressed seeing her talking to him.

'Just get me a coffee.'

A sense of disappointment touched Jim momentarily. He had hoped that everything would go nice and smoothly when he arrived in Ellsworth. But already things seemed to be going wrong. First his hoped-for job seemed to have disappeared with the death of the previous marshal; and now Rose had reacted strangely when her father entered the room. As if she believed that he wouldn't approve of Jim.

*Well, he'll just have to learn to approve of me,* thought Jim, *because I ain't giving her up easily.*

Rose left him for a few moments to get his coffee before returning, cup in hand.

'There you go,' she said. She leaned close to him as she passed him the drink. 'Meet me outside in half an hour,' she whispered softly into Jim's ear before turning away from him and preparing another drink. As Jim lifted his coffee to his mouth his sense of disappointment left him as quickly as it had arrived.

Boland's watcher hadn't moved from his position by the wall, and had also refused to take his eyes off Jim. *Well, well, Jim Boland. I think I'd give up cattle driving for a sweetheart like her too,* he thought.

Rose came towards him, whiskey held in his direction.

'Thanks, missy. Mind if I ask you a question?'

Rose paused for a moment, considering the stranger's request. 'Depends what kind of question it is.'

The stranger chuckled. 'Don't worry, ma'am. It's nothing sinister.'

Rose nodded her head slightly, indicating that he should proceed.

'I was just wondering who that feller is you're so friendly with?'

Rose waited an instant, considering her answer. She crooked a finger at the stranger indicating to him to come closer, which he did. They were now so close that he could even smell the subtle, flowery scent of her perfume. Her lips parted as she began to speak.

'None of your dang business!' she snarled as she poured the whiskey down his shirt.

The stranger didn't even move as Rose walked away, having once again rendered him speechless. The same drunken cowboy who had spoken to him earlier began again.

'Sure is feisty, ain't she?' he sniggered, his face appearing as if it were one big smile.

'Sure is,' agreed the stranger wryly, looking down at his whiskey-soaked shirtfront.

★　★　★

Jim sat at the bar, watching Rose flit through the crowd like a butterfly in the middle of a nest of spiders. Gradually, the minutes ticked by, the time for them to meet outside coming ever closer. At last, Jim could stand the waiting no longer and decided to step outside. He rose and picked his way through the crowd, moving towards the door, unaware that the eyes of his follower were on him all the while. He turned to see if he could spot Rose and walked straight into a table full of both professional gamblers and drunken cowboys. He sprawled head first on to the table, his outstretched arms sweeping bottles, glasses, cards and money to the ground. Those who were sitting at the table jumped to their feet just as he fell into their midst.

'What the? Goldurn! What d'you think you're doing?' asked a tall card-sharp, patting down his ruffled black suit as he stared at Jim spread-eagled on the floor.

'You're after ruining our faro,' shouted another character with a fearsome growl. His face was thick with stubble and his hair slick with sweat. His grey shirt was open exposing his thick, muscled chest. 'And I was just about to win big!' he continued, his voice sounding ominous now, the words hissing out from between his gritted teeth.

'Take it easy, Baker, I'm sure he didn't mean it,' said the man in the suit soothingly. Looking up from his position on the floor the only thing Jim noticed about the threatening figure standing over him was his hands' proximity to his shooters.

'Now, come on, feller, take it easy. It

was an accident, I wasn't looking where I was going,' Jim pleaded. He pushed himself up from the ground with one hand and, having regained his feet, stood opposite the man who was complaining. All the while, Jim kept his eyes on the other man's hands.

'Well, I'd better teach you to watch your step, feller,' he said to Jim.

The saloon hushed, all eyes on the two men eyeballing each other.

'Take it easy, now, don't do anything stupid,' Jim appealed.

'The only feller who did something stupid was you when you wrecked our game!' The gambler's hand flashed to his side but Boland was faster. Fingers pressed triggers just fractions of a second apart. The room reverberated with the din of firing handguns. When the smoke cleared there was just one man standing — and that man was Jim Boland. Just as his adversary had fired, Boland had flung himself to one side and pulled the trigger, hitting the man opposite in the upper thigh. Boland now stood over the stricken cowboy. His teeth were still gritted but this time it was a groan of pain that escaped from between them.

'Someone get a doctor,' Jim called. 'You're going to be all right, it's only a nick.' As Jim stared at his injured foe he noticed a change in the man's face, his eyes flickering momentarily as if looking over Jim's shoulder. Instinctively, Jim plunged forward just as the flashing steel of the blade of a Bowie knife sped by his right ear as he was attacked from behind. Instantly there was, once again, the report of a gun being fired. A body thumped to the floor. Lifeless. The body wasn't Jim's, however, and neither had he fired the gun. He stood over the dead man; the knife was now lying beside his lifeless hand.

*I'm making some enemies tonight,* Jim thought.

There was something about the dead man that seemed familiar. He looked behind him at the man he had wounded and saw tears in his eyes. Then Jim realized that the two men were brothers!

*Time to get out of here, I don't like how this evening is going one little bit!*

Jim strode quickly out of the saloon, not giving any thought as to who had shot his would-be killer, and past the crowd, who had begun drinking again as if nothing had happened. All the while, however, he kept his hands hovering over his holsters and his eyes peeled. At last, he made it out the door and took a sharp intake of breath as the cool of the evening hit him. He looked up and down the street but nothing moved. Satisfied that he had the area to himself, he sat down on the wooden boardwalk. He took off his hat and ran his fingers through his hair, letting a long breath escape his lungs.

'You sure do know how to make an entrance, pardner.' The voice froze the blood in Jim's veins.

*They have the drop on me,* he thought. *Stupid! I should have been more careful.*

'I was just minding my own business when some fellers tried to make some trouble. You'd better not try doing the same or you'll end up just like them!'

'I know that you didn't shoot that second jigger. Whoever did sure saved your bacon.'

*Dang, this feller has me here. He must have been watching inside. Better try and distract him.*

Jim turned towards the shadows, searching for the source of the voice.

'Why don't you show yourself, feller? You wearing a bad suit or something?'

The voice chuckled. 'I think if I showed myself you'd shoot me down. You should be more careful with them hogs of yours if you plan to stay here permanently, Jim Boland.'

*Hotdang, he knows I'm planning on staying and he knows who I am, too!*

Jim didn't like this situation one little bit. He had been in tight squeezes before but never this tight, with him up against an invisible opponent who knew everything about him, and he knowing nothing in return.

'You seem to know a lot about me, feller. How's about you tell me something about yourself to help even the score?'

'I can tell you that I like the look of that little lady of yours!'

This struck a chord deep within Jim. He had left Rose a year before with great effort, worked hard to earn enough money to get back to her, and now that he was back his life was under threat, and maybe even hers too. He decided to take a chance. He slid his left hand on to his hip and gripped the butt of his gun. He had taken a chance that this side was hidden from his opponent in the gloom. Then, after a moment, seeing that he was still alive, he assumed that the chance had been worth taking.

Then the voice began again. 'Now, Jim, don't go thinking about shooting me. I can see your hand on that gun.'

Boland cursed softly and took his hand away.

'I don't think that that's a nice way to be treating the feller who just saved your life in that there saloon.'

*So this was the feller who had shot the jigger with the knife, but why?*

'What did you do that for?'

'Isn't that what partners do for each other?'

Jim was confused. 'But I don't have a . . . '

The sound of boot on wood indicated that Jim's saviour and adversary all rolled into one was about to reveal himself. Jim wasn't sure what kind of a prank was being played on him, but whatever it was, he wasn't enjoying it. Had this man saved his life in the bar just so he could end it himself? And what did he mean about being his partner? Once again, Jim Boland's arms tensed as he prepared to draw his six-shooters if needed.

The first he saw of the emerging figure was the brim of his wide hat. Next he made out black-leather boots with white tips, then a long black coat covering a white shirt and dark pants. It wasn't the stranger's clothes that shocked Jim Boland into dropping his hands from his guns, it was his smiling face.

'Howdy, partner,' said Harry McIntyre, grinning.

# 10

Jim yawned loudly and rubbed the sleep from his eyes. Quickly, he stopped himself from making any more noise in case he woke the figure asleep in the adjacent bunk. Too late.

'Morning, Jim.'

'Morning, Harry.'

Jim's mind wandered back to the night before, remembering how Harry McIntyre had nearly scared him half to death. And then, more important, how he had found out that it had been Harry who saved his life in the bar. He had given Harry a good roasting for the trick he had pulled on him, quickly followed by a grudging thanks for saving his life. He and Harry had been given a room in Rose's father's saloon for the time being, until Jim got on his feet.

As they settled into their lodgings,

the night before, Harry had asked him how he had met someone as pretty as Rose, seeing that he had previously told Harry that he had been so unsociable. Jim had thought long and hard before answering.

'Well, Harry. Some would call it blind luck, but I prefer to call it fate.' Jim went on to tell Harry the full story.

'Last year we were riding to Ellsworth, for my first time ever, because of the circulars sent down by the *Ellsworth Reporter* newspaper saying that Abilene was dying as a cowtown. When we got to the outskirts of the town everybody was very excited, seeing that it was most of the fellers' first time being there. We headed into town once we had been paid off, looking for fun. I went first to get a haircut and a shave before going to buy some new boots; my old ones were worn through. I figured that I'd have more chance of drink and such like in these unfamiliar saloons, you see, if I dressed up rather than if I looked like my usual messy self.

'Well, I hit the town hard. I was drinking and drinking and drinking until I eventually ended up here, in the Southern Belle. The last thing I remember of that night is downing whiskey after whiskey. The next thing I know is I'm being poked in my side and some pretty young thing, Rose as it turns out, is shouting at me to get up. I guess I must have fallen asleep on the floor. She just kept on at me, trying to get me up. Eventually I struggled to my feet and stared into her eyes for the first time. I ain't ashamed to admit it, Harry, I fell in love immediately. That sweet, sweet face, long flowing hair and those deep-blue eyes. It was as if they could cut right through me. See right into my soul. I can tell you something, Harry, I never sobered up so quickly in my life.

'I managed to secure a room in the saloon for the rest of my stay in Ellsworth, a week in total, but I have to say I didn't spend much time in the room. I spent all my time following

95

Rose around, trying to get her attention. One night I got my chance at last to get close to her. The saloon was packed as another few herds had come in during the day and Rose's father was sick with something. I volunteered to help and I suppose they were so desperate they agreed! I never worked so hard as I did that night, Harry. I was nice as pie to every single feller that came in, no matter what they said to me. I was on my very best behaviour. That was until some jigger started messing with Rose. She was serving him in the far end of the saloon and I was wondering what was keeping her so long.

'Well, I looked down and saw this feller and his friend being rough with her, pushing her around and such like. I could feel the anger rising up inside me, filling me like boiling water fills a kettle. That anger quickly changed to fear, however, when I saw them trying to drag her out the door. I was now just a few yards from them and I lunged at them. As I leapt through the air I caught one of the jiggers on the head with a bottle of liquor I was holding. I landed beside the feller holding Rose. He looked so shocked at my sudden appearance that his jaw was nearly scraping off the ground. Just because he was surprised didn't mean that I was going to show him any mercy though. I drew back my right arm and landed a hook square on his jaw, knocking him out cold.

'As I stood there looking at the two jiggers lying on the ground I noticed for the first time the look on Rose's face. I didn't know how she was going to react. Was she as frightened of me as she had been of them because of my violent actions? Did she think of me as a troublemaker, just as many other people did? I prayed not. And my prayers were answered. She half-walked to me, half-collapsed into my arms. I helped her back behind the bar and sat her down. I couldn't talk to her just then as the customers were looking for liquor again now that their entertainment was over.

'When at last I managed to get back to her she looked a lot better. The colour had come back into her cheeks and the sparkle returned to her eyes. She thanked me over and over again for what I had done but I told her not to mention it. I asked her to be quiet for a minute and told her my feelings for her, unable to hold them back. How I thought — no, how I was sure I loved her. Loved the way she looked, the way she walked and the way she talked. I must have rambled on and on because in the end she asked me to stop as I was making her blush. I was petrified as she sat there in silence. I was more frightened waiting to hear whether she felt the same about me than if I'd been cornered by a crazed steer. Then those beautiful red lips moved.

' 'Jim,' she said, 'them sure are some nice things you just said, but I don't think I deserve to have them said about me.' She waved away my protests before continuing. 'I like you, Jim, I really do. I don't know you that well, but I can tell that you're a good man. But I don't know if anything can happen. I mean you're a cowboy, and I can't leave Pa here by himself.'

' 'Rose,' I said, 'if I told you that I'd give up my life as a cowboy and stay here with you would that make you happy?' I could tell that something had stirred deep within her. She leapt forward from her chair and embraced me passionately.

' 'I remember seeing you the first night you came in here, falling around drunk and the like. And I remember picking you off the floor the next morning and thinking what a state you were in. Then, when you came down the next night you were a different man. You didn't drink or nothing. At first I thought you were sick from the night before, but then you came down the next night, and the next, and you still didn't drink. I could feel your eyes on me, Jim Boland. And I looked back at you too, except you didn't see me. I desperately wanted you to be a good man, to forget about that first night. But I just can't. My pa says, 'Once a drunk always a drunk.''

'I pleaded and pleaded with her to give me a chance. I think she must have seen something in me, about how desperate I was to be with her. She came around and we made a pact. I'd leave the next day with the rest of the fellers and head back down the trail. I'd work harder than I ever had before and make some money to get by here when I made it back, until I found a regular job. And that we'd stay in touch, somehow. I sent her a letter every week of that year I was away, and let me tell you, it was the hardest year of my life. Her face was in front of me every night before I went to sleep, in my dreams all night, and she was the first thing I thought of every morning when I woke up. I haven't touched liquor in a whole year. I've walked away from more troublemakers trying to rile me than I can keep count. The thought of getting back to Rose kept me going all the time. Rose's letters gave me the will and the strength to help me through the tough times. And now I'm back here, and all my plans are up in smoke!'

# 11

'What d'you mean Jim?'

He explained to Harry how the recently deceased marshal had been persuaded to sort out work for Jim by Rose's earnest lobbying. But now that he had been gunned down, everything had been thrown up in the air. Silence reigned in the room for a while. Jim had by now swung himself out of bed, his legs in his red long johns hanging over the side of the bed.

'I'm sure something'll turn up, Jim,' Harry offered.

'Yup, I sure hope so,' Jim replied, his voice full of doubt.

He began to get dressed. First, he pulled on his heavy grey woollen trousers over his long johns. Next, his worn, frayed shirt was swung on to his back and his braces fastened over them. To finish he tied his bandanna around his neck and grabbed his gunbelt from the chest of drawers beside the bed. Harry watched all this impassively until something Jim did caught his attention. Boland reached into the top drawer of the chest of drawers and pulled out a small leather pouch with a piece of string attached. Jim saw Harry's inquisitive look but said nothing. He lifted the string over his head before slipping it around his neck. The pouch dangled from the makeshift chain, and rested against his chest. He slipped it inside his shirt.

'Interesting piece of jewellery you've got there,' Harry said jokingly, trying hard to hide his curiosity. The look that crossed Jim's face as soon as he heard Harry's comment made him wish he had kept his mouth shut, however. Jim now wore such a melancholy expression that Harry knew he would have been better keeping his thoughts to himself.

'I'm sorry, Jim, I didn't mean to . . . '

Jim just ignored him and buckled his gunbelt.

'Time for breakfast, I think,' Harry mumbled to himself, eager to dispel the tension in the room.

Harry led Jim down the stairs, the wooden steps resounding under their hard-soled boots. As they reached the bottom they were confronted by an imposing figure. Harry sidled by the man with the glaring eyes, nodding his greetings as he went. As he made his way down the corridor he was relieved that it was Jim and not himself who would have to deal with him, friend or not. Cole faced up to Jim as he reached the bottom of the stairs.

'So, you've come back for her,' he began. 'I thought I'd seen the last of you when you rode out of here last year. You're not the first cowboy to have fallen for her, you know. But I'll give you one thing: you're the first to come back clean and sober — like you promised you would.'

'Well,' Jim replied, 'that's all because of your daughter, Mr. McCormack. If it wasn't for her I'd probably be dead in a ditch somewhere, I'm not afraid to admit that. I'm no angel, but I'm willing to do whatever it takes to make Rose happy, and to make you believe that I'm worthy of her.'

Rose's father took a step back so that he could get a better look at Jim. He was very protective of his only child; his wife had died young and he hadn't remarried, but he also knew that someday he would have to hand Rose over to another man. But he had promised himself one thing a long time ago — he would never let Rose marry a cowboy!

'If you're serious about her you'll do me one thing.'

'Anything,' Jim blurted.

'You'll give up riding the trail. I don't want my daughter lying in bed at night thinking about where you might be or what high jinks you might be getting up to. You got to settle down here, in Ellsworth. Earn a decent living. That's all I ask. When I first saw you I didn't like you, Boland. But Rose obviously sees something in you. At least, judging from your shooting last night you'll be able to protect her. This is a dangerous town and a pretty girl like Rose gets a lot of unwanted attention. My trigger finger is getting a bit rusty, Jim.' His voice sounded wistful, as if he pined for days gone by, simpler times as he thought of them. 'Maybe you can look after her for me.' He bowed his head. He had said his piece. He knew Jim wasn't a bad feller, but it didn't make the possible loss of his daughter any easier.

'I ain't a child, you know!' called a voice from the adjoining room. Rose had been listening to their conversation all along. 'I am able to mind myself, Pop. I'm not the baby you think I am.' She came through the doorway and stood facing them, hands on hips. 'And I'll decide if I want to marry someone; you won't trade me like a side of beef! I have a mind of my own. And anyway, I don't even know if I want to marry this jigger or not!'

With that she turned and strode away from the two men, leaving them dumbfounded in her wake. 'Just like her mother,' Cole whispered, a wry smile on his face. 'Come on, let's get some breakfast.'

# 12

Jim wasn't entirely happy with the plan Rose had suggested over breakfast, and the more he thought about it the less sure he was that he wanted to go through with it. He was stuck, however. If he was to stay in Ellsworth with Rose he would have to find a job. Rose had suggested a solution and now he was following it up, as he had promised her he would. Although he half-hoped it wouldn't prove successful.

As he walked into the marshal's office he felt that same feeling as he had the first time he had seen Jake Bradman. He wished he could turn and walk out through the door again, but this time Bradman had seen him silhouetted against the street outside.

'Come in, citizen,' Bradman called loudly. 'What can I do for you?'

Jim stepped into the dark room and

took off his hat. Bradman sat in shadow, so that his face remained hidden; only his tone of voice gave Jim a clue to his emotions.

'Howdy, Marshal. My name is Jim Boland,' Jim was surprised at how timid he sounded. It seemed as if his voice was muffled by the blanket of black that covered the marshal's office.

'Ah, the sharpshooter from the Southern Belle.'

Jim was taken aback, he hadn't thought that news of the previous night's incident was widespread.

'Don't look so surprised, I am the marshal, after all. It's my job to know what goes on in my town.'

'Of course. I didn't mean any trouble last night,' Jim replied. He was nervous now.

The last thing he wanted was to be a marked man as he tried to build his new life. He was frightened that his dream would be snatched away from him now that he was so close to making it happen.

'I know you didn't,' Bradman replied. 'They were just two drunks. Shooting them saved me a job later on! You've nothing to worry about from me.'

Jim breathed a sigh of relief. Bradman's words soothed him a little and put him more at ease. 'Can I help you with anything else?' Bradman asked, wondering why Jim was still standing in his doorway.

'It's just that I'd been promised a job by the feller you've replaced,' Jim told him. 'I suppose now that he's gone, so is the job,' he added wistfully.

'Now don't be so sure,' Bradman replied. 'I don't know what job he had in mind for you before he got in the way of a bullet or ten, but I sure can find something for you to do. I ain't got no deputy and I sure could use someone with a steady hand like yours to help me keep order in this place. What d'you say?' Bradman rose dramatically to his feet and held out his hand toward Jim.

Jim didn't know how to react. He

had been apprehensive about going to see Bradman, a man who evoked an unexplainable feeling of suspicion and wariness in him, and now he was being offered a chance to work alongside him! As far as he could see, he didn't exactly have many options open to him; there weren't that many opportunities in society for cattle herders who took early retirement. If he wanted to stay in Ellsworth he would have to bite the bullet. He clasped Bradman's hand with his own.

'Looking forward to working with you,' he said.

Rose was overjoyed when she heard Jim's news. Deputy Jim Boland! That had a very dignified ring to it. Jim thought he even saw a look of grudging admiration in Cole's eyes too, although he couldn't be sure of it. Something nagged at him, however. He still didn't trust Bradman; there was something about him that irked Jim, but the smile on Rose's face convinced him that what he was doing was right, and that he could put his suspicions to one side for the time being.

Jim's happiness was tempered, however, by some bad news about Harry. Jim rushed into the room where both he and Harry had slept the night before and in there found the town doctor standing over one of the beds. In it lay the figure of Harry McIntyre, his eyes closed and his breathing shallow.

'What happened, Doctor?' Jim asked, unable to keep the fear from his voice. He didn't even notice Rose slipping into the room behind him.

'He was down at the stockyards, watching the cattle getting loaded. A bull broke free . . . ' Rose answered him before the doctor could speak. Jim turned to her, afraid of what she might say next, ' . . . and ran right over him.'

Jim went cold. He turned to the doctor. 'Doc?' he whispered.

'Hard to tell,' the doctor replied. 'He's going to need a lot of care. He has a few broken ribs, a big bang on the head and God only knows what else is going on inside him. He's out cold, I don't know whether he'll come out of it. He might recover, he might not. Who knows in this town? Keep him comfortable, that's the best you can do for the time being. I'll be back in a few days to check on him.'

After the doctor had left Jim sat by Harry's bed, unsure of what to do, what to say. 'He'll be OK, Jim,' Rose whispered. 'I'll make sure of it. He can stay here, Pa said.'

'Thanks,' Jim muttered. They left the room together, Jim patting Harry gently on the head before they went.

★   ★   ★

The sound of shouting on the street outside woke Jim the next day. By the time he had pulled on his clothes and gone out to see who was causing all the commotion a small crowd had gathered around an elderly man who was sitting on a horse-drawn cart.

'Where's the marshal?' the man was

shouting. He had a frantic look in his eyes and his mop of grey hair was unkempt.

'I'm his deputy,' Jim called. 'What's the problem?'

'It's rustlers,' the man replied, drawing a gasp from the crowd around him. 'They've stolen my cattle. I woke up this morning and rode out to check on them. Except there was none to check. Just a few of the old ones who aren't any good to anyone.'

'Now take it easy,' Jim said, trying to take some of the heat out of the situation. The crowd around him were getting more and more agitated and he knew that if they got out of control innocent blood could be spilled. Posses were not known for their powers of restraint when it came to seeking out perpetrators of crimes. Personal grievances often overrode the aim of correctly resolving a criminal situation.

'What's going on?' boomed Bradman's voice. In the growing disturbance Jim hadn't seen him approach. He quickly explained the facts to the marshal.

'Cattle rustlers, you say?' repeated Bradman. 'And they struck last night?' The farmer nodded in reply.

'What ya going to do about it?' someone in the crowd yelled. 'It could be any of our cattle next.'

'Don't worry,' Bradman proclaimed, his voice so forceful that it quietened the murmur of the crowd. 'My deputy and I will get to the bottom of this. In fact, I think I know very well who is responsible for this terrible act of thievery.' He turned to the farmer. 'You'll have your cattle back by tonight.'

The crowd cheered as the marshal finished speaking. He beckoned for Jim to follow him as he headed for where their horses were tethered. All in all it was a very impressive performance from Bradman, Jim thought. In fact, he had nearly convinced Jim himself that his previous doubts about him were misplaced. Until, that was, they reached their destination, and Bradman's true nature would come to the fore.

# 13

Jim and Jake rode out of Ellsworth, Jake leading the way. Jim's attempts at conversation were met with grunts from Bradman. No information was forthcoming from the marshal and Jim quickly gave up trying to engage him. Bradman's silence only served to increase Jim's suspicions. No matter how hard he tried he couldn't warm to Jake. His gut instinct was one of wariness, and Jim tended to trust his instincts. They had been right about Rose and he felt that he should follow them now too.

As they rode across the grassy plain outside Ellsworth Jim couldn't stop himself from thinking about the life he had left behind. The freedom, the lack of responsibilty, the predictability. But that was over, and he wasn't exactly happy with where he found himself now. So much seemed right; he had a job, he was near Rose, he had a place to stay. But all was not well. He didn't want to admit it; he tried to banish such thoughts from his mind, but he wondered whether he was making a mistake. He loved Rose all right, but he wasn't used to committing so much to one cause. He usually chose the line of least resistance, the easy way out: ride trail, get paid, drink until he passed out, get another job to buy more liquor. The circle of life according to Jim Boland. And he was now beginning to wonder whether it wasn't such a bad philosophy to live by, as he rode into an unknown situation with a man he didn't trust.

They crested a hill and rode slowly down to the farmstead that lay in the valley below. The sun was high in the Kansas sky, now, and the riders' shadows played across the carpet of green that stretched all around them. A cool breeze crossed the plain, taking the edge off the sun's heat. The setting was idyllic, but the drama to be played out was a tragic one.

Jim patted Jesse gently on the forehead as he hitched him to the wooden railing outside the farmhouse. 'Keep your eyes open, partner,' he said softly. 'I need you to watch my back.' There were bits of debris scattered around the yard in front of the house. Firewood lay on the ground half-chopped and a chair lay overturned outside the door.

Bradman pounded on the door and shouted: 'This is the marshal. Anyone in?' No response. He hammered again, louder this time, and more violently. Still no answer. Bradman shoved the door open and strode inside with Jim following closely behind.

The house was dark inside, little of the sunlight had seeped through the dirty windows. The air within the house was heavy and oppressive. It was as if a cloud of fetid air filled the building. It made the house seem stale, lifeless and unwelcoming. Jim instinctively put his hand on the butt of his gun, removed it when he realized what he had done, but then replaced it once more. He was on edge; the silence in the house was fraying his nerves.

They moved slowly through to the kitchen. Rotting food covered the table, broken bottles lay on the floor. They continued into a small hall: here darkness hung over everything, making it seem even smaller. It seemed to Jim that the very walls of the house were closing in on him. Two doors led off the hall: two bedrooms, Jim assumed. Bradman paused for a moment and held up his hand. Jim stopped behind him, holding his breath. A low, droning sound could be heard from behind the nearest door. This time Bradman drew his gun too. With a violent thrust of his right boot he kicked in the door and charged into the room.

Jim was taken aback by the abject figure they found. The room smelled of foul air and stale alcohol and whoever was inside here hadn't washed much in the last few days. A single bed lay against one wall; lying on it, so dishevelled that Jim wasn't sure whether it was a person or a collection of old bedclothes, was the man Bradman had come to see. Jim holstered his gun, he wasn't going to need it against this forlorn figure. Bradman put away his weapon, too, and picked his way across the room to the bed. He caught hold of the sleeping figure and shook him roughly.

'Get up, you good for nothing. I want to talk to you,' he barked. He beckoned to Jim to come over. The man in the bed cursed under his breath, reluctant to wake up and furious at being disturbed. He was groggy and bleary eyed.

'Catch him, Jim,' said Bradman. 'Let's get him out into the light. Let's see what we're dealing with.' They dragged the man from the house, his language getting worse as they went. Jim was surprised at how feebly he struggled. His main resistance came from his invective, not his limbs.

*It's as if he's weak or hurt, somehow,* Jim thought.

120

'It's like dragging a newborn calf,' Jim said to Bradman.

'Except a newborn calf wouldn't smell this bad,' Bradman replied. He wrenched the man from Jim's grasp and flung him out through the front door. Jim glanced quickly at him, unable to hide the look of shock and anger in his eyes.

*This bag of bones doesn't need to be roughed up, not by the law, anyhow,* Jim thought.

As he emerged into the light it took Jim a moment to adjust to the brightness. 'You!' said the man on the ground, his voice sending a chill through Jim. The voice was laden with malice and malevolence. Slowly, Jim focused on the unshaven, washed-out face, contorted by anger. He looked familiar, but from where? 'So,' the man continued, 'you killed my brother and now you're back to finish me off?'

It was then that Jim recognized him as the drunk from the Southern Belle, the man whose brother had tried to kill him. Baker was his name. Bradman looked at Jim to see his reaction, but his expression was unmoving. His stolid face hid the turmoil he was experiencing within.

# 14

Jim glared at Bradman but all he got in return was an icy stare. He was on his own.

'First you kill my brother and now you want to kill me? Is that it?' the farmer asked. Jim was unable to reply immediately, he was too stunned by the turn events had taken.

'Shut up,' Bradman said menacingly. 'You know why we're here.'

It was as if the man had noticed Bradman for the first time; all his attention had previously been focused on Jim.

*Just the way Bradman wanted it*, Jim thought.

'No, Marshal, I don't know why you're here,' the man replied. 'Especially not with this crook,' he pointed at Jim. Bradman kicked out violently, striking the grounded man in the ribs.

'Don't talk about my deputy like that,' he growled. He turned to Jim. 'Get him on his feet.' Baker didn't offer much resistance as Jim dragged him from the ground. Jim found him surprisingly light; very little flesh seemed to cover his bony frame. A low moan escaped from him as Jim gripped him and there was a patch of red on his breeches where his gunshot wound had started bleeding again. The gunshot wound that Jim had inflicted.

'Maybe we should take it easy on this feller,' Jim said. 'He's in pretty bad shape.'

'What?' Bradman barked. 'I'm not paid to give criminals an easy ride. There's nothing wrong with this jigger. At least nothing he didn't bring on himself.' Bradman drew back his fist but Jim stepped between him and their captive. 'Give him a break, Marshal. We need him to be able to talk, don't we? No point beating him and turning him against us?'

Bradman disagreed, Jim could tell,

but there weren't going to be any more random acts of brutality while he was around. At least not if he could help it. Jim had morals, and ethics, believe it or not, even if some of them were buried pretty deep inside him. Some hadn't seen the light of day for so long that they would be blinded if they got a glimpse of the outside world. But there was something about seeing a defenceless man being abused that triggered something inside Jim. Suddenly, he wasn't sure whether he was siding with his marshal or the broken man he held in his arms.

'All right, all right,' Bradman blustered. He caught Baker by the shirt. He raised the sunken face up roughly, causing the man to wince with pain once more. 'We hear you're rustling cattle again, Baker,' Bradman spat out, venom in his voice. 'If you come clean and show us where you have them, we might go easy on you.' Baker looked first at Jim and then at Bradman, an incredulous smile on his face.

'That's why you're here? You fellers think I've been stealing cattle?' A low rumble began within him, spread through his body and emerged from his mouth as a coughing, cackling laugh. 'That's the most ridiculous thing I've ever heard,' he hacked. 'I never had much faith in lawmen but you two fellers are the best ever,' he said sarcastically.

What happened next happened so quickly that Jim didn't even have time to react. All he knew was that Baker was lying on the ground, blood oozing from the corner of his mouth. Bradman had a lightning-fast right hook, and Baker had just felt the force of it. The marshal glared at Jim as if challenging him to question his methods again. This time Jim kept his mouth shut.

'Get him up again,' roared Bradman. Jim did as he was told. 'Now, do I have to ask you again? Show us your cattle, or . . . ' Bradman left the sentence hanging in the air, the silence more menacing than any words could be.

'All right,' Baker replied.

Jim noticed a change in Baker, it was as if he had sobered up, or had at least recovered most of his wits. The gravity of the situation now seemed to be dawning on him. There was another change, too. Earlier, he had been indignant, awkward and stubborn. Now, his eyes displayed only one emotion — fear.

'I ain't left this house for the last three days,' he pleaded. 'When were these cattle supposed to have been stolen?'

'Never you mind,' Bradman muttered.

'It's just that . . . ' This time Baker turned to Jim, imploring him to listen, to see that he was telling the truth.

*How quickly things change,* thought Jim, *when he sees me as an ally so soon after thinking I came here to kill him. Bradman sure does have a way with people,* he concluded.

'It's just that I've been sleeping and drinking and sleeping some more since my brother died. I mean, what am I supposed to do now? The two of us worked this farm with our father before and when he died we worked it together. Just the two of us. And now there's just me. How am I going to cope? I just don't know,' he finished in a small voice, so quiet that Jim could barely hear it.

They mounted their horses, Baker climbing on to Jesse with Jim. Jim couldn't help but feel sympathy for Baker. In some way he reminded him of himself. But he had a job to do now, and he had a responsibility to Rose to do it properly so that he could stay in Ellsworth. As they set out he said a silent prayer that they wouldn't find any stolen cattle on Baker's land.

They continued on in silence across the grassy plain until grazing cattle came into view. It was a sight that carried Jim back. The brown, beefy animals moved slowly across the plain, grazing peacefully as they went. This whole experience: riding across the plain, the smell of Jesse, and the cattle, all reminded Jim of his past life. But it also reminded him of Rose, for whom he had given it all up. Or, more accurately, who had saved him from it.

*Let's get this over with,* he thought. *Time to get moving.*

He spurred Jesse on to where the cattle were grazing. Bradman had to urge his mount on to catch up with this sudden movement from Jim. For the first time, Jim felt as if he was directing matters. He felt as if he had assumed some control. But he had underestimated Bradman, and the lengths he would go to get his way.

# 15

Jim reined in Jesse as they reached the grazing cattle. Both he and Baker had dismounted by the time Bradman arrived a few moments later, pulling vigorously on his reins as he stopped just short of them. Baker stood meekly with his head lowered, but Jim met his marshal's glare dead on. Bradman wasn't happy with him, that much was obvious. Jim's show of independent action had been both unexpected and unwelcome. But, Bradman reasoned, it only gave him another opportunity to show him who was boss. He had liked Jim, at first. He had thought he could rely on him, that he would do as he was told. And of course, there was the other reason he had hired him. The reason he would one day tell to Jim, and with great relish. But the time wasn't right, yet. He would wait. It would be worth it. But now he was beginning to have second thoughts about his deputy, and that couldn't be good news for Jim.

Bradman dismounted from his horse, his gunbelt rattling as he hit the ground.

'These your cattle, Baker?' he asked with a sneer.

'Sure,' Baker replied. 'They got my brand on them, don't they?'

'Let's take a look and find out,' said Bradman. He strode over to Jim and grabbed Baker from beside him. He held him roughly by the shoulder and half-dragged, half-marched the limping man towards some cattle grazing close by. They scattered as the men drew nearer, Bradman's noisy approach spooking them.

'How many cattle you got?' asked Bradman.

'Five hundred head. Not much, but it was always enough for the two of us,' Baker replied.

'Must have been difficult to make a living with just five hundred cattle, now. Mustn't it?'

'What are you trying to say?' Baker questioned, bridling at Bradman's tone. 'I just said that we had enough, didn't I?'

'Only asking, that's all.'

Jim listened intently to Bradman's barbs. He was trying to bait Baker, to get him to react. That much was obvious to Jim, and it seemed as if Baker was falling into his trap.

Bradman walked to the nearest steer, calling soothingly to it. He left Baker behind him, his wounded leg having got the better of him. Bradman's way with cattle seemed to be as effective as his way with people, it seemed, as the animal bucked his head once before galloping off, kicking up his hind legs as he went

*This feller certainly has no feel for cattle*, Jim thought, *he frightened it half to death*.

'Hey, Jim!' Bradman called, 'You're good with these beasts, aren't you? You must be, after living with them for most of your life. Am I right?'

'Sure, Marshal,' Jim replied. He was taken aback by Bradman's tone of voice; it was almost friendly, conciliatory.

*I'm your best buddy now that you need me to do something for you*, he thought.

'Grab me a steer and check its brand. I'd like to get back to town some time tonight.'

*Amen to that.*

As he edged closer to the nearest animal it seemed to Jim as if Bradman's comment had been true; he had spent most of his life with beeves. At least he could understand animals, or, at least, understand them better than he could humans. They made their intentions plain, if a bull was going to charge he'd start pawing the ground, bellowing, put his head down and run. And if you didn't get out of the way you were in big trouble. It was different with people. They injured in different ways. A sly comment here, a contemptuous look there. Jim preferred it when he was

133

being dealt with out straight, when all the cards were on the table. But Jake Bradman was a man who wouldn't even tell whether he was playing the game or not, never mind show his hand.

'Easy, pet,' Jim whispered as he rubbed the coarse brown flank of the steer.

*The sooner I make sure that these are Baker's cattle the sooner this whole thing will be over with*, he thought.

'Hey,' Jim called, rubbing the animal all the while, 'what's your brand, Baker?'

'B bar K,' came the reply. Jim froze; it felt as if all his energy had suddenly been yanked from his body.

'What's the brand on the cow, Boland?' Bradman called harshly. Was there a hint of a note of triumph in his voice? Jim couldn't be sure. In fact, Jim couldn't be sure of anything any more.

'Boland! Didn't you hear me? What's the brand?'

'Circle A,' Jim replied, his voice

barely carrying to the marshal.

Bradman leered cruelly at Baker. There was no mistaking it, he was happy with Jim's answer. 'How's about that?' he said, sneering again at the farmer.

'It can't be, there must be some mistake!' Baker stammered. He looked wildly about him. 'Check the other cattle, maybe that one strayed here.'

'The man who's cattle was taken uses that brand. He lives ten miles from here, on the other side of town. I don't think a dumb animal would stray that far unless it was driven. Unless it was stolen.'

Baker's head dropped; he was over-whelmed by the whole situation. He couldn't comprehend what was happening to him, neither did he realize the seriousness of the crime. If Bradman thought him guilty of rustling, which he obviously did, he was likely to be hanged, a fate that was drawing closer by the second.

Baker looked up again, a lost look in

his eyes. 'I-I just don't know.' The death of his brother, the shock of being assaulted by the marshal, stolen cattle being found on his land — it was as if he had just given up all attempts at defending himself. He was a beaten man; he no longer knew whether he was innocent or guilty. Jim empathized with the emotion he saw in Baker. He knew what it was like suddenly to be left alone, with no hope in sight. But Jim had survived his crisis while Baker looked as if he would be suffocated by his.

'I don't understand,' he pleaded again.

'Maybe we should check some more of the cattle,' Jim said. 'See if any more of them have different brands.'

'One stolen animal is the same as a thousand,' Bradman barked. He glared at Jim from the corner of his good eye. 'You don't believe he's guilty, do you?' he spat.

Jim stayed silent.

'What is it? Do you feel some sort of

sympathy for him because your buddy killed his brother? Well this jigger's no angel, let me assure you of that. Are you, Baker?'

Unsurprisingly, the farmer didn't respond, he was barely aware of what was going on about him now.

'About two years ago you and your brother stole some money from a feller in town, didn't you?' Bradman spoke to Baker loudly, as if he were chastizing a slow child. 'I was told you fellers were trouble when I came here. Looks like the reports were right.'

'We were drunk,' Baker replied morosely. 'We didn't know what we were doing.'

'Yeah, and when that feller turned up dead couple of days later? You had nothing to do with that either I suppose?'

'We did not!' The fire had returned to Baker's voice now, stoked by the memory of the events of two years previously. 'We were found innocent.

That feller was a drunk and he was probably killed by another drunk. But not by me or my brother, and that's the truth! We were just in the wrong place at the wrong time.'

'For some reason I don't believe you,' Bradman teased. 'I never did put much stock in the word of a drunken criminal.'

'You better watch your tongue, marshal or not!' Baker hissed as he moved threateningly towards Bradman. The air was thick with menace.

*This isn't going to end well,* thought Jim.

'D'you hear that, Jim?' Bradman taunted. 'This jigger is telling me, Marshal Jake Bradman, to hold my tongue. Well I never!' Bradman coughed out a derisive laugh. 'No wonder your good-for-nothing brother got himself killed with a temper like that!'

Baker's hand flashed inside his shirt and a moment later the sound of a single shot filled the air. Baker slumped to the ground, dead.

A chilling smile crossed Jake Bradman's face. 'Good shot,' he said to Jim. 'You just saved my life.' Jim holstered his pistol automatically, overcome by an overwhelming feeling of emptiness.

# 16

## Laredo, Texas

Ella was exhausted, both physically and mentally and her throat burned from lack of water. Ever since she had slipped away from the ranch she knew that what she was undertaking was laden with danger. But she had no other choice, of that she was certain. He had driven her to this. She steadied herself as she stood on the porch of the wooden homestead. She didn't know how she would be received, but it couldn't be any worse than going back would be.

She knocked hard on the door and waited impatiently. She could hear the sound of footsteps coming towards the closed door and moments later it was opened slowly, just wide enough for the person inside to peer out. There was a pause as she was studied from within before the door was flung open and the barrel of a rifle was thrust in her face.

'What do you want?' came the voice from inside the door. 'This some kind of trap or something?'

She gathered herself before speaking. 'I want to make a deal,' she said. 'I can get him for you, at a price.'

They all sat around the table: Ella, Charlie MacWhirr, and his three sons Thomas, Alvin and John. If Mike could only see me now, Ella thought, I'd be a dead woman.

'How do we know you're telling us the truth?' Alvin, the eldest brother, asked. 'Maybe he'll be waiting for us, kill us all?'

'He doesn't care about you fellers any more,' Ella said brutally. 'He's stolen all your cattle, he controls the trade with Mexico here. To him, you don't even exist any more. I'm here because I want out. That ranch is like a prison. The only reason I'm out now is because he's got another woman with him. I can't take it any more, I need money and you're the only people I can come to. I need to get home, need to get away from here.'

'We don't have that much money left,' Charlie answered. 'He's nearly broke us.'

'What's he worth to you?' she asked him. 'What's it worth to you to get your town back? I reckon it's worth everything you've got left.'

\* \* \*

There were three men as usual posted on the perimeter of the homestead, guarding the property and person of the most powerful man in Laredo, the man who had violently seized the power he now wielded for profit at the expense of the other townsfolk. Ella sauntered out to the lackey who stood guard at the main gateway to the homestead. She swung her hips alluringly under her cotton shift, aware of the power she had over the tired, cold man who stood before her. In her hands she held a mug of coffee. 'Hey Chet,' she called softly, 'you keeping well?'

'Sure am, Ella,' he replied, keeping a close eye on her as she approached. His eyes were drawn to her, his focus distracted from his guard duties.

'Brought you some coffee,' she said sweetly.

'Mighty kind of you,' he responded. She came right up close to him before she handed him the mug. He could smell her fragrant aroma; almost feel the heat of her body. So entranced was he by her presence that he didn't notice Thomas MacWhirr approach him from behind. MacWhirr raised his revolver by the barrel and brought the butt down on the back of the guard's head, knocking him out cold. This performance was repeated with the two other watchmen before three shadows moved in through the gaps left by the unconscious sentries.

Minutes later their target was dragged from his bed and clubbed across the back of the head with the butt of a Winchester. The three brothers bound him and dragged him from the house. A wagon charged along the path leading up to the house and pulled up before them. The prone figure was flung in the back. Before pulling off, the MacWhirrs fired some rags doused in paraffin into the barn and bunkhouse. As they sped away the ranch burned.

Ella had fled as soon as she saw the wagon leave. She had to get to the rendezvous and also avoid being questioned about why she hadn't raised the alarm when the man she was supposed to be in bed with was kidnapped. What Ella could not have seen, however, were Costello and Lopez emerging from the bunkhouse as the fire took hold. They left the fire to spread. Getting their boss back was the priority.

'The MacWhirrs,' Lopez hissed. Two of the guards ran up to him, their hands to their bloodied heads.

'We never saw — '

'Shut up,' Lopez shouted. 'I should

kill you both right now.' His hand flashed to his side and the two guards flinched. 'Get the others,' he ordered, 'and try and put out the fire.' The guards ran off, glad not to be riddled with holes.

'You,' Lopez pointed at Mason, 'come with us. And bring the dynamite.'

The three men rode off, leaving the flames from the fire lighting up the sky behind them.

'We can cut them off on the plain. They'll have to stick to the track through these hills with the wagon,' Costello shouted.

'We'll get them,' Lopez prophesied. 'And they'll be sorry for what they've done.'

They took off cross-country over the ragged hills that surrounded the ranch, trying desperately to get in front of the fleeing wagon before it reached the MacWhirr homestead.

★ ★ ★

The ropes dug deep into his wrists. Each time the wagon hammered over a rut in the road another layer of skin chafed from them. Clouds of dust rose from the wheels of the wagon as they sped along and the sweat from the two black horses driving it foamed freely. The three MacWhirr brothers sat in the wagon with him, Alvin and John opposite and Thomas alongside. Alvin's upper lip rose into a sneer, drawing the skin even tighter over his bony face.

'The great Mike Bradman,' he snarled. 'Not so great now, eh?' The other two brothers broke into derisive laughter. Mike stared at the grinning, leering face opposite. He hated these people. Hated that they had power over him; that they were in control. He had been conducting a running battle against them for control of the small town of Laredo and the profitable smuggling trade across the Mexican border. It now looked as if he had lost that fight. The wagon jolted once more and the restraints dug deeper. Mike lowered his head and stared at the floor of the wagon, refusing to look at the sneering faces surrounding him.

*   *   *

Pete Mason lurked in the doorway of an abandoned saloon. The street was dark, sinister. The only light was from the lamps hanging from the oncoming wagon, gradually growing larger as they drew nearer. They illuminated the dishevelled, dilapidated wooden buildings bordering the street. The buildings were windowless and crumbling, most of them were derelict and deserted. This was a dead town, forgotten about. Business had moved elsewhere and the people had followed. Mason was the only person there and he was only there because he was waiting for the wagon.

He reached his hand inside his coat and drew out a match. In one swift movement he sparked it against the sole of his boot and brought it to the cigarette in his lips. The wagon shot past his hiding-place, the dust kicked up by its passing causing him to cover his mouth with his gloved hand. He spat out the cigarette, quenched by the dust. He waited. Nobody else was following. He walked around the side of the saloon, quickly mounted his horse and set off in pursuit of the speeding wagon.

The wagon left the town behind and headed out into the barren, dusty plain. The driver and the man sitting alongside him up front were hands on the MacWhirrs' farm and not used to this kind of action. They spent most of their time riding around the ranch, not transporting bound prisoners at high speed.

'I hate this place,' the driver roared, his voice barely audible over the beating of the horse's hooves and the churning of the wagon's wheels.

'The sooner we get rid of this feller the better,' his companion agreed.

'This place always spooks me,' the driver continued. 'I almost expect a ghost to walk out in front of us.'

The man next to him just nodded solemnly in reply. His finger unthinkingly reached for the trigger of his Winchester. 'I'll be glad to finish this trip, and that's for sure.' Tired of shouting, he finished the sentence in a whisper, 'Everything out here is either dead or fixing to die.'

There were at least two figures alive on the plain that night, however. Lee Costello and Hernan Lopez lay in wait for the wagon. They sat on their steeds, a little way back from the roadway, hidden in the inky black shadows. 'Not much longer now,' Costello muttered, trying to keep the nervousness from his voice.

'I'd say about five minutes, judging by the lamps,' Lopez replied. Lopez was much older than Costello and more experienced in what was about to happen next. Lopez smoked his cigarette vigorously, his cheeks hollowing as he inhaled. There was a wild look in his eyes, Costello thought. Lopez reminded him of an animal. He possessed a willingness to go to any lengths to get the job done. He was unpredictable, and that was what frightened Costello the most.

'If they have hurt him, if they have so much as broken a hair on his head . . .' Lopez muttered malevolently.

'Take it easy, Hernan,' Costello soothed. 'Let's just get him back first. Then we can make them pay.'

Lopez turned towards Costello. The tip of his cigarette lit up the only part of Lopez's face that Costello could see, but even so there was no mistaking the violent anger in his expression and his tone of voice.

'Take it easy?' he hissed. 'The boss saved your life, saved my life too. When you were in the depths of hell, being shot at from all angles, you didn't think twice about the boss's offer. He got us out of there. He gave my family a home, what's left of them. What he has asked of us is in return is nothing compared to what he has given us.' He paused a moment to gather his breath before continuing. 'So no, Costello. I will not take it easy!'

Lopez's outburst quietened Costello.

'And may God help those pigs who have him. Because no matter how loudly they squeal no one will come to help them if they have hurt him.'

Costello was eager to change the subject, to calm Lopez, but he couldn't summon the strength to say anything. He seemed paralysed, his mind already casting back to that day nine years ago.

'Remember, Costello? Remember what he did for you? I'll never forget what he did for me, and that's for sure.' Lopez finished his cigarette and flung it to the dusty ground. 'Not long now,' he said. The wagon was drawing nearer. The end was coming. The MacWhirrs were in for some surprises.

'Ready?' Lopez asked. Costello nodded in reply before realizing that Lopez couldn't see him in the darkness. He forced out a strangled-sounding 'Yes.'

'All right,' Lopez replied.

Lopez spurred his horse across the road and assumed his position opposite Costello. Costello sat low in the saddle. He felt exposed although it was unlikely that he would be spotted in the pitch blackness. At least, not until it was too late for those in the wagon. He hated these moments. Alone. Waiting. The calm before the storm. It was just like when he was in the war, except the pay was better now. Violence and killing.

It hadn't always been like this, but he had seen and done things during the war that no man should have to live through. It had changed him. Made him into the man he was today. The violent, unthinking thug taking orders from an animal like Lopez. He didn't allow himself to dwell on those memories, those brutalities that had steered his life down this path.

He returned his attention to the dark plain. He could hear the rumbling of the wagon's wheels and the beating of the horses' hoofs as they approached. He wiped a film of sweat from his brow with his dusty-gloved hand, leaving a dark smear across his forehead. He knew that, no matter how hard he tried, he could never shake the imprint of those days from his conscience.

But he had a job to do now. He had to bust free the man who saved his life that day. He didn't contemplate deeply what kind of a life he had been leading since Bradman and Lopez had intervened. He just simply did what he had to do to stay alive. He would be forever in their debt; that he knew. But maybe this would help ease the load a little.

The wagon was almost upon them. Lopez waited somewhere on the opposite side of the road. He would have to wait for Lopez to act first, to begin the attack. Waiting. Always waiting.

An explosion filled the air. To the wagon driver and his colleague it appeared as if the roadway had disappeared before their very eyes. Dust coated the air and the sound of falling rubble was audible from every side. The horses reared up, terror in their bulging eyes. The driver did not have time to try and calm them, however. Lopez leapt from the darkness and landed beside the driver. His knife was in his hand and he drew it across the driver's throat. The driver's companion trained his gun on Lopez. Before he could fire, however, Costello grabbed him from behind and stabbed him in the heart. All this had happened in a matter of seconds.

'I thought you were going to let him shoot me,' Lopez muttered. Costello just smiled grimly back at him. They quickly cut the terrified horses loose and the wagon ground to a halt. Inside, Bradman lay still, listening to the commotion.

Alvin MacWhirr held his hand to his head as blood streamed from a cut over his eye. 'Damn it,' he cried, 'what's going on out there?' He stuck his head through the door and called into the night.

'What's after happening? Everything all right?'

'Rock falls,' Lopez called back. 'Spooked the horses. They're trying to break free. Could use a hand fixing them up again.'

Alvin cursed and handed his rifle across to John. As he went to the back of the wagon and prepared to jump down Thomas called to him. 'You know we're not supposed to get out until we get there.'

'You want the horses to break away and have to walk the rest of the way?'

John nodded in glum agreement. 'I'll give you a hand,' he muttered. Bradman was still on the floor, feigning unconsciousness. If they had seen the faint smile that crossed his lips, however, they would never have dared leave that wagon.

John and Alvin stepped down on to the dusty track. The lamps were out and their eyes struggled to adapt to the darkness. They edged forward in single file, using the side of the wagon as a guide.

'Hey, fellers — ' Alvin's call was strangled in his throat as a gun butt

155

cracked down against his head. A fraction of a second later and John received the same treatment. Thomas, the only brother still conscious, heard Alvin's aborted cry inside in the wagon. Sweat dripped into his eyes, causing him to blink frantically. Bradman could almost smell the young man's fear inside in the belly of the wagon. Thomas gripped his revolver tightly.

'Fellers?' he called out. 'Alvin? John?' His voice was shrill, his throat constricted with fear.

'Why don't you come on out here and join us?' Lopez's voice, dripping with menace caused Thomas' breath to catch.

'Dear Lord,' he exclaimed and crossed himself furiously.

'Don't try to be a hero,' Lopez continued. 'If I have to go in there and get you it won't be pretty.' His speech was casual, and was all the more deadly for it.

'One left,' Costello muttered. 'There's always one.'

'Line them up,' Lopez ordered Costello. Costello grabbed Alvin and John and shook them roughly back to life. He dragged them to their knees and placed them beside each other. They were groggy but conscious and their moans of pain filled the night air.

Inside in the wagon, Thomas steeled himself. He had to take action. Costello and Lopez watched as a head gradually emerged through the door of the carriage. Lopez's hand tightened on his revolver. The head was Bradman's with the barrel of a gun planted firmly against the back of it. The same knowing smile was on Bradman's face. As if he knew how this would all turn out.

'Drop your guns, fellers,' said Thomas firmly, affecting an air of bravado. Still, Bradman wore that same expression, ignoring the feel of the cold steel against his skull.

'I don't think so,' Costello replied. 'There's two of us and only one of you. How about you drop your piece and we just about might let you live.'

'Very funny,' Thomas growled.

Costello was growing anxious in case someone should come upon them. The longer they stayed in the open the more chance that the operation could take an unexpected turn.

If all was going to plan, Mason was watching the roadway the wagon had travelled. But the sooner this situation was resolved the better. Time for some definite action.

'Drop your guns or your boss gets it,' Thomas said impatiently. He pushed the barrel of his gun hard against the back of Bradman's head, forcing him to lurch forward.

Costello walked away from both Bradman and Thomas MacWhirr, catching them by surprise. He put his revolver to Alvin's temple.

'No. Please,' Alvin whimpered.

Costello never took his eyes off Thomas. 'Let him go or I'll kill your brother.'

'You wouldn't,' Thomas said quietly.

The air reverberated with the sound of a single shot.

'Good Lord . . . ' Thomas whispered. Bradman stumbled forward as the grip on him was loosened. Once again Costello's weapon spat death and a bullet passed through Thomas's forehead. He collapsed to the ground, dead.

Costello helped Bradman to his feet and quickly unshackled him. He helped him on to the back of his horse before he mounted in front of him. He turned to Lopez and pointed to the remaining brother, John, who was lying on the ground. He was shocked, terrified and disorientated.

'No witnesses, all right?' Costello said. Bradman smiled once more.

Lopez pulled the trigger and finished the job.

# 17

Ella was waiting. It was getting dark and she knew something was amiss, that something had gone wrong. But she still had hope. Maybe he was just running late. Maybe . . .

This was the meeting point, of that she was certain. She just wanted to get her money and get out of there. She had been totally beholden to Mike Bradman. He had not been her husband. He was never going to marry her, she had realized that eventually. She had been attracted by his power and his influence as well as his charisma. But that attraction had waned when she learned that she was just another of his pretty possessions. She had left her home, left a worried father and mother behind and for what? She had lost her self-respect, her independence and her identity. That was why she was now hiding in this cold, dark abandoned homestead. She had had to get out. And now she was waiting for the last piece of the puzzle to fall into place — money that could give her hope and a chance to go back north. Home.

Anxiety consumed her as she lay shivering in the shadows. Had she been abandoned by the MacWhirrs, just as Bradman had abandoned her? Or worse, had her part in the abduction been discovered? She shuddered to think what would happen to her if Lopez got his hands on her now.

Night began to fall and the cold that came with it advanced slowly but steadily, chilling her to her core. Her teeth chattered, the flimsy dress she wore providing no protection against the elements. She hadn't planned on being out in the open for this long. She had presumed that she would be long gone from the area by now, with her horse and reward money provided by the MacWhirrs.

'Something's wrong,' she whispered. The very uttering of the words crystallized her fear. She rose and made for the barn. At least there might be some shelter inside the building. The sound of a horse approaching stalled her, however. Relief flooded through her, salvation was near.

She turned to greet the horseman as he drew closer. She could make out from the rider's bulky shape that it was Charlie MacWhirr, father of the three brothers. He pulled his horse to a sudden halt before her. Dust rose from its hoofs, causing Ella to raise her hand to shield her eyes.

'You're late,' she cried, trying hard to conceal the anxiety in her voice. MacWhirr didn't answer.

'I said, you're late!' she repeated.

Still there was no answer from the rider. The dust settled, so that Ella could see him clearly. Her breath caught and a cold chill ran through her. His eyes were red and the foam on the horse's flanks were proof that they had ridden at a hard gallop.

'What's wrong?' she asked, already knowing that she would receive an answer that she did not want to hear.

'You!' His voice dripped with venom, malevolence punctuating every word. 'You betrayed them.'

She couldn't respond, her words stuck in her throat. She felt as though she couldn't breathe, as though her windpipe had contracted, stopping air from reaching her lungs.

'What are you talking about?' Her voice was like a whimper, barely audible. Her self-preservation instincts were kicking in even as she spoke, however. She was looking for a way out.

'They're dead,' he howled. 'They're all dead!' His anguished cry filled the air like that of a wounded wolf. The pain of the death of his boys overwhelmed him and rendered him incapable of rational thought. Someone had to pay for their deaths and Ella appeared the most convenient target.

'You scheming whore. You tricked my

boys. You led them into a trap,' he roared.

Ella searched frantically for an escape, her mind working rapidly as she glanced about her. The brothers were dead; Bradman was free; her life was over. She was going to be killed by Charlie MacWhirr if she stayed here, and by Bradman if she ran back to him. There seemed to be no way out, but Ella was a resourceful woman.

MacWhirr reached into his saddle holster for his Winchester. Ella ran, not waiting for him to draw it from its sheath. A shot rang out behind her and a bullet flew past her ear, cutting through her flying hair. She turned the corner of the barn and ran along its side. She had to get inside, had to get some cover.

There was a small door halfway along the side of the building. She reached it and slammed into it, trying to force it open. She cut her knuckles as she pounded against the worn wooden door. It wouldn't budge. MacWhirr came round the corner of the barn, on foot now.

'Come back here,' he cried. 'Pay for what you've done to me and my boys.'

She pushed hard against the door once again. She was growing frantic now. He was drawing closer, just twenty feet away and closing. He levelled the gun at her once more. With a primal yell she flung herself against the door one last time, just as MacWhirr's finger tightened on the trigger. The rotten wood crumpled under her determined charge and she fell to the ground inside the barn. MacWhirr's bullet whizzed harmlessly past the doorway.

He approached the opening quickly, frustrated by how long it was taking him to finish off this slip of a girl. Caution was not a factor for MacWhirr. He was blinded by sadness, rage and alcohol. He charged in the door, roaring for Ella's blood. He stopped dead however, and his hand dropped to his side, his gun smashing to the floor. He looked surprised, even shocked, Ella

165

thought. Slowly, the realization of what had just happened to him dawned on MacWhirr. He looked down at the handle of the pitchfork protruding from his belly, with Ella, lying on her back, holding the end of it. She pushed hard again, forcing the tines deeper into his internal organs, tearing at his heart. Slowly, like a falling tree, he slumped to the ground. As Ella picked his gun from the ground she saw the life fade from his eyes.

She rifled through his pockets but found no money. She took his coat and left the barn. She jumped on his horse and didn't look back as she rode swiftly away.

# 18

The three riders came to a stop, far from the scene of the slaughter. They dismounted from their horses and Bradman drank greedily from Costello's canteen.

'You all right, boss?' Lopez asked eagerly.

'Fine,' Bradman replied between gulps. 'Good work fellers.' Lopez beamed with satisfaction while Costello just nodded in reply.

'Where to?' Costello asked.

'Back to the ranch,' Bradman replied.

'Back to the ranch? But it's probably burned to the ground,' Lopez exclaimed.

Bradman shot him a steely look from beneath his bushy black eyebrows.

'He said to go back to the ranch,' Costello intervened. 'So we go back to the ranch.'

They mounted up once more, Lopez

swallowing his bile. Costello had better be careful, talking to him like that.

An hour later they were sitting in the remains of the bunkhouse. The guards had split; the only one still around was Mason. The four men watched the embers of the barn and the ranchhouse glow in the early-morning light.

'How did they get past the guards?' Bradman asked at last. Mason mustered up the courage to tell of the incidents with Ella.

'Why would she do that, though?' Lopez asked. 'She was well looked after here.'

'Why do women do anything?' Bradman questioned in reply. 'Maybe she was bored? Maybe she took a fancy to one of them brothers? Maybe their pop?' Again, he smiled. Again, nobody responded. 'All that matters is that she betrayed me. The little whore!' He spat the words from his mouth, his neck muscles so tight that they looked like lengths of coiled rope. 'We've got to find her and teach her a lesson.'

'She could be miles away from here by now,' Costello replied. 'She could be anywhere.'

'I don't think so,' Bradman said. 'She can't survive by herself without help. She's heading for home but she'll have to stop for the night. There's only one place she can be: Fort Worth. If we hurry up we'll get there before she moves on.'

'But there's lawmen in Fort Worth,' Lopez pointed out.

'I don't care,' Bradman hissed. 'I want my Ella back so I can teach her a lesson.'

Costello refused to allow himself to think of what lesson Bradman meant to teach Ella. He knew that once Bradman's anger was aroused it wasn't easily sated.

'In Fort Worth she can use her talents to get whatever she wants,' Bradman mused. 'I'm sure of it. That's where she's headed,' he added with an air of finality. 'And so are we.'

★ ★ ★

Later that day the four horsemen rode into Fort Worth. They didn't make a grand entrance by strolling down the centre of Main Street but crept in by a back way, staying in the shadows all the while. Bradman, aware that his face was known in every lawman's office in the county, had his hat pulled down over his eyes. He waited outside the hotel as Costello went in and booked a ground-floor room. Bradman then went round to the back of the building and waited for Costello to open the window to allow him in. Waiting for him was a bottle of whiskey and a glass.

'Search every corner of this god-forsaken town and don't come back until you find her,' were his last words before he began to drink. Costello, Lopez and Mason left the building to begin the hunt.

★  ★  ★

Ella's horse was exhausted as she rode into town. She led him to the water trough and he drank deeply, the cool water soothing his burning throat. Ella didn't enjoy wearing a good animal out like that but it had been necessary. She had had to put distance between herself and Bradman, and now she must lie low. She hadn't met anyone on the journey and had ridden hard all the way. Amongst people now, she felt safer, even though she still had no money. Food and a place to rest were her first priorities.

She caught sight of herself in the window of a gunshop. Dishevelled, scattered hair, a dust-covered face and filthy dress was what she saw. Not the appearance she was used to seeing in the mirror. 'We'll have to do something about that,' she murmured to herself.

She went back to the water trough. 'Push over,' she said to her horse. 'My turn.' She splashed water on her hands and face and then on her hair. Running her hands through her hair she slicked it down and pushed it back, regaining some control over it. She checked her reflection in the water. 'A little better,' she muttered. At least now she looked clean.

She left the trough behind and made for the nearest saloon. She did not go in straight away but waited in the shadow of the awning, watching people coming and going. She didn't have to wait very long before she made her move, however. She stepped from the darkness and rushed forward. All the while she kept her head down but her eyes fixed forward, taking in all around her. She moved fast and slammed headlong into a middle-aged man about to enter the saloon.

'Sorry,' he exclaimed as she careered into him. 'I'm very sorry, ma'am. I didn't see you there.' She looked up at him with large, sad, eyes. Eyes that seemed to burrow into his heart. 'Are you all right miss? Is something the matter?' he asked concernedly.

She gazed at him, seemingly unwilling to speak.

'It's all right,' he said. 'If something's

wrong, you can tell me.' His tone was kindly and he drew Ella out.

'I was on my way here to do some business when I was set upon by some varmints. They took my wagon and all my money.' Tears welled up in her eyes and her voice quivered. She put her arm on his as if to support herself.

'That's terrible,' he exclaimed. 'Are you hurt?'

'No,' she replied. 'But I sure got a terrible shock.'

'I'm sure you did.' He couldn't take his eyes off her angelic face. She was making him feel as if he were her protector, her saviour. And he was more than willing to play that part. 'We'd better go to the marshal and report it. Maybe they can be caught.'

'I've already done that,' she lied.

'All right.' He fell silent. 'Is there is anything I can do to help?'

'Well, I don't like to ask.'

'No, please. Anything.'

'I am awfully hungry and thirsty, and

like I said, they made off with my money and all.'

'Say no more,' he cried. 'Leave it to me.'

Ella allowed herself a small smile as she put her arm through his and walked with him into the saloon.

★   ★   ★

Lopez, Costello and Mason had split up so as to cover more ground. It was time-consuming to explore every street, side street and alleyway. Costello's boots resounded on the boardwalk as he made his way past shops that had closed for the evening. Night was falling and there weren't many people about on the streets. The sound of a saloon up ahead called to him, tempted him. He was tired, hungry and cold. One whiskey couldn't do any harm, surely?

He pushed the swing doors apart and strode into the saloon. It was busy, the tables full of card-players, drinkers and diners. He made his way to the counter and called for a whiskey. As he drank he put his back to the counter in order to survey the crowd. He couldn't really care less whether they found Ella or not. In fact, he didn't see how they could find her. She might not even be in Fort Worth, although he did admit to himself that Bradman knew her better than he did. Bradman had only himself to blame too, he thought. If he had a girl like that he wouldn't be messing around in honky-tonks. He'd keep her all to himself, wouldn't give her an excuse to try and slit his throat.

The whiskey went down quickly and well and he called for another. It arrived and he turned to face the crowd again. A couple were rising from their table in a corner of the room but he decided to stay at the bar. The man was considerably older than his companion, as far as he could tell from looking at the girl's back, and she sure wasn't acting as if she was his daughter! Lucky feller, Costello thought. He smiled to himself. But the expression froze on his face as he saw the girl pass outside the saloon window. It was Ella.

She saw Costello drop his drink and lunge forward. She had been careless and she cursed herself for her slackness. Everything had been going so well. Her partner had become extremely excited at her desire to see his home. Little did he know that it had been Costello's arrival in the saloon that had sparked that desire. The older man stumbled along. Ella had been plying him with drink all evening, paid for by himself of course, in order to gain total control over him, but this only meant that he moved sluggishly and clumsily.

'Old fool!' she shouted as she ripped his wallet from his jacket pocket before shoving him off the boardwalk and into the street. She had set off at a sprint before he had realized what had happened. Costello's boots were pounding on the boards behind her.

She darted to her left and shot down an alleyway. Her breath came sharp and shallow. The exertions of the last couple of days were taking their toll on her but she had to keep going. The alternative didn't bear consideration. She turned quickly up another alleyway, ducking and weaving as she went, trying desperately to lose her pursuer. She didn't dare look behind her. She knew he was there, knew that he wouldn't let her go without a real fight. She didn't know where she was going, however. She only recognized that she must somehow lose herself in this warren of alleyways or else find herself a horse and get out of town as quickly as possible.

Costello chased hard, eager to bring the matter to a resolution, but Ella remained elusive. Every time he turned a corner she was just disappearing around the next. Where the hell were Lopez and Mason anyway? he wondered. Probably in a saloon or a dance-hall. He knew that wasn't likely, though, particularly as regarded Lopez. His loyalty to Bradman was unwavering. Whatever might have happened to

Mason, Lopez was certainly still out searching. Little does she know, he thought, that she would be better off if I caught her rather than Lopez.

She ran down a narrow street, exhaustion making her legs feel leaden. There were buildings close to her on both sides. To her right were the rear of a row of buildings while those on her left showed her their fronts. There was no boardwalk on this street, just hard-packed dust. For the first time she turned her head to see how close Costello was. Her concentration wavered and she fell face first on to the dirt, her foot having gone into a rut. She tried frantically to get to her feet but her ankle couldn't take any weight. She yelped in pain, the sound coming involuntarily from her mouth. Costello appeared at the end of the alleyway. He glanced to his left at first, the opposite direction to Ella's prone figure. She still had not been spotted. She dragged herself into the shadow beneath a window, making herself as small as possible. She knew, however, that it was only a matter of time before she was discovered.

She heard the window above her head open.

'In here, quick,' came a hissed voice. Her heart leapt. Salvation beckoned. Strong hands dragged her up and in through the window. She collapsed on to the floor of the room, fighting hard to control her breathing.

'Thank you, sir,' she gasped. 'You saved my life.' She looked up and her heart skipped a beat. She was staring into the grinning face of Mike Bradman.

Ella lay on the bed, her ankle strapped up with bandages in makeshift fashion. Anger burned in her eyes as she looked around the room at the four men. Lopez, Mason and Costello stood leaning against the walls while Bradman sat on a chair next to her bed. His elbows rested on his knees as he leaned in close to her. She could smell his alcohol- and smoke-tinged breath as he spoke to her. She wondered how she had ever found this man attractive.

'My little butterfly,' he began. 'My pretty little Ella.' His voice was soft and tender. Ella knew that it was just an act. 'Did I not treat you well? Didn't I do everything you asked of me? Didn't I give you everything you wanted?'

Ella pursed her lips and stayed silent. Better not to speak and rouse his anger. He was well capable of that by himself without any assistance.

'Why? That's all I want to know. Tell me what I did wrong. I can change.' Again, he had that tender, loving look on his face, like a lover pleading for forgiveness. She didn't take the bait. 'Tell me what I did that you would give me up for dead!' His shout rang round the room, causing Costello, Lopez and Mason to start. Here it is, Ella thought. The storm is about to break.

'Were you in love with one of the MacWhirrs? Is that it? Would you have preferred a pigsty as a bed rather than the luxury I kept you in? Or maybe you wanted to share your bed with all of them? Maybe you wanted a different MacWhirr every night?' Silence filled the air. 'Well?'

This time Ella was taken aback, the force of Bradman's voice terrifying her. She gradually regained her composure.

'It doesn't matter what I say,' she replied, her voice low but strong. 'You're going to kill me, anyway.'

Bradman chuckled as he stood up and walked away from her.

'You don't deserve to die. Do you think those animals would have killed me right away? Do you think they would have put me out of my misery like a wounded horse?'

She knew exactly what the brothers had planned for Bradman. She had known it when she had sold him out, but she had not cared about it. Her blood now ran cold, however. She had not expected her actions to come back on her like this. She had hoped to be far from here by now. Hoped to have been well on her way home, but luck had not been kind to her. She now lay on a bed in this dingy hotel room. Immobile and in pain, and under the influence of the man she had sold out to be tortured and killed.

'Keep an eye on her, fellers,' Bradman said. 'I'm going out for a short while. There's a feller here owes me a favour. Watch her,' he continued. 'She's like a viper, get too close and she'll kill you.'

★ ★ ★

Ella slept fitfully, exhausted by her exertions and from the pain in her ankle. When she awoke Bradman had returned. Both he and Costello brought her out of the hotel and put her in the back of a covered wagon. She slumped on to the floor, her bad leg out-stretched. Bradman told Mason to stay in the back of the wagon to watch her. Lopez sat up front while Bradman and Costello mounted their own horses.

'Things have got a little hot around

here,' he said to Costello. 'I'm fixing to head north. You coming?'

Even though Bradman had phrased it as a question, Costello knew that there was only one answer.

'Yes,' he replied.

'Good.' Bradman nodded. He didn't even bother to ask Lopez, so sure was he of his loyalty.

The wagon rolled out with the two horsemen riding before it. In the back Ella gritted her teeth as her ankle jarred against the wooden boards. Eventually she passed out. She was heading northwards at last, but not the way she had planned.

# 19

He rode into town by himself, leaving the others just outside the limits. He would be back for them, provided everything was as he hoped. His skin was as brown as the dry, dusty landscape he had travelled through, a brutal, rocky landscape which had been dominated by the harsh edges of mesas and buttes that bore witness to his eviction. He moved amongst them as between a line of guards, their watchful gaze making sure that he left their territory.

He took a swig of the last of the water from his canteen and then rubbed his mouth with the back of his hand. He hadn't shaved for a week and the rough stubble grazed his hand. The water refreshed him, the cool liquid soothing his parched throat. He walked on, crossing into the outskirts of the town.

He walked in the middle of the dirt track. The roadway was deserted except for a couple of mongrels panned out in the morning sun, tongues drooping to the ground. Ellsworth was a town that woke up late.

He was hungry and thirsty so he made his way into a saloon. It was empty but for the burly man behind the counter.

'Howdy stranger,' the barman called.

'Howdy yourself,' he replied. 'Whiskey.'

He downed the contents of the glass in one and ordered another.

'You sure are thirsty,' the barman commented.

The stranger growled, as a wild animal would. 'Just pour.'

A woman joined the man behind the bar. She immediately caught the stranger's attention. He watched the way she moved, the sway of her hips, the shape of her legs beneath her dress. He made a note to come back later, when his business was done.

Ellsworth was just like any other town he had passed through. It just happened that Ellsworth hadn't begun to die, yet. It hadn't yet been bled to death by the parasites that seemed to suck the life from every cattle town he visited — but it was only a matter of time. Even in the prime of life death can be just around the corner. Even at the peak of health there can be evidence of decay, and the stranger was on his way to visit one of those agents who could bring about that very decay.

★　★　★

Jim didn't speak on the ride back. He had killed a man, an innocent man. Baker had been unarmed and had been merely reaching inside his coat for a flask of liquor he had kept hidden there. They had buried the body out on the plain, Jim working without thinking, covering Baker's body bit by bit with earth. It felt as if he was killing him all over again, smothering him with dirt.

186

What would he tell Rose? What would she think of him? He wondered if killing changes a man. Was he a different being now that he had taken a life and, if so, would Rose notice the change? Maybe she wouldn't want to be with this man, this killer? Jim rode on, deep in thought.

★   ★   ★

The stranger left the saloon and strolled down the town. He walked in the middle of the road once more, eschewing the shade of the wooden walkway. He had a better view from the street, he would be ready if anyone tried to get the drop on him. Dust rose around his heels as he walked, covering his boots with a film of grime and dirt. He looked important, walking down the middle of town with a small cloud of yellow dust trailing him. In fact, he was just a hungry man come to town to collect what was his. He knew where he was going but he was in no hurry to get there. He rehearsed in his head what he might say or do to the man he sought. He had done something to him once before, many years ago, but he didn't think that that would be necessary today. But if things didn't go as he hoped . . .

His boots resounded on the walkway as he stepped up off the street. He paused outside the open door and drew a deep breath of warm, humid air. It was time to get what he came for, to collect what he was owed. He strode purposefully into the room. All his preparations had been unnecessary, however. The room was empty. He sat down behind the large, wooden desk that dominated the space and waited.

★　★　★

'You know where to find me,' Jim said to Bradman when they got back to town.

'Sure,' the marshal replied. 'And, thanks again!' The marshal smiled without warmth. Jim felt sick as he stared at Bradman's hateful expression. He walked Jesse over to the saloon and stabled him out back. He spent a long time grooming the horse; the slow, rhythmic movements gradually regulating the frantic beating of his heart. When he felt he was ready to face Rose he patted Jesse one last time and headed for the saloon. He had made up his mind to tell her what had happened, the whole story, and to explain how it hadn't been his fault. But when he saw Rose's expectant face he knew that he couldn't. He went upstairs to Harry instead and told the whole story to his unconscious friend.

Bradman still wore his disingenuous smile as he strolled back to his office. He chuckled as he thought of how he had manipulated Jim, how he had reasserted his control over him. He stopped on the threshold and his right hand flashed to his holster.

'I don't think so, Jake,' said the stranger.

Bradman froze. He thought about running but something in the stranger's voice stopped him. 'Mike?' he asked tentatively. The rumbling laughter that filled the room and reverberated around the small office told him that he had guessed right. The stranger, Mike, rose from his seat and walked to Jake. They embraced, pounding each other on the back and laughing some more.

'Welcome, brother,' said Jake.

# 20

'What're you running from now?' asked Jake. He poured another glass of whiskey for himself and Mike and they drank them down in one swallow. They were sitting in the front of the lawhouse, the setting sun shining softly through the half-open door.

'The usual,' Mike replied. 'Rustled some cattle and some fellers got angry. They tried to kill me, brother,' he added wistfully. 'They tried to kill me.' He took another drink. 'Where are you living?' Mike asked.

'Just here at the minute. Small room upstairs,' Jake replied.

'I've got some fellers with me, this place is too small for us all. You got any ideas?' Jake was silent for a moment. 'There's a ranch that's just been recently vacated,' he said with a smile.

Later that night the doors to the

saloon swung open so violently that they slammed hard against the wall inside.

'Howdy Marshal,' called Rose's father from behind the counter, 'what can I get you?' The saloon was busy and Jake and Mike pushed their way to the counter, bumping and jostling anyone who got in their way. They were still there three hours later, still drinking whiskey. Rose watched them from behind the counter, serving them only when she had to, eager to avoid their drunken leering. But the saloon was busy and both Jake and Mike were drinking so much that she had to serve them many times.

'So,' Jake said to Mike, 'why are you hanging on to that hussy if she tried to kill you? If it was me I'd have run her through long ago.'

'I know, I know,' Mike answered. 'I just can't seem to do it. Anyway, she's handy to have around, I figure, when we get set up again. She can keep the place clean and tidy, at least. We'll definitely have to get another cook, though.' They both laughed at this before downing their drinks.

'Well, there sure are plenty of easy women in this town who you can replace her with,' Jake said. 'This place sure is a hell-hole.'

'Hey, at least it's your hell-hole,' Mike replied.

'No, brother. Now it's our hell-hole.' They clinked glasses before Jake continued: 'Let's enjoy tonight and tomorrow we can really set about bleeding this place dry.'

They both cheered at this and drank again.

Jim came into the bar to talk to Rose.

'You all right?' she asked. 'You look like you've seen a ghost.'

'I'm fine', he answered. They couldn't talk now, the saloon was too busy. And Jim had just spotted Jake. He walked over to the marshal.

'Who's looking after the office?' he asked.

'My hero!' Jake exclaimed, ignoring Jim's question. He was well on the way to being flaming drunk by now. 'This man,' he said, turning to his brother, 'saved my life today.'

'You did?' Mike asked, turning to Jim. Without waiting for an answer he continued,

'Well, I sure am grateful. I don't know what I'd do without my little brother.' He draped his arm over Jake's shoulders and pulled him close.

'Your little brother?' Jim asked incredulously.

'Yep,' Jake replied. 'This handsome feller is my brother Mike.'

'Nice to meet you,' said Mike as he extended his hand to Jim.

'Mike, this is my deputy, Jim Boland,' Jake explained to his brother. Jim grasped Mike's hand and gave it a firm shake.

'Nice to meet you,' he mumbled.

Jim felt uneasy. One Bradman in town was bad enough, but two could mean nothing but trouble. Jim's concern showed on his face.

'Don't look so worried, Jim,' Jake

jibed. 'You'll still be my deputy. Mike is more in the cattle trade, you might say. Isn't that right, Mike?' They laughed complicitly.

'Anyway,' the marshal went on, 'I'm not sure I could find someone who's such a fine shot as yourself, Jim.' He mimicked the firing of a gun with his fingers. 'Bang! This feller can outdraw a flask of liquor at ten paces better than any man I know.' Mike and Jake descended into laughter at Jim's expense. Jim drifted away from them, leaving them to their revelry.

Eventually, after what seemed like the longest night of his life, the saloon emptied out and Jim and Rose got a chance to speak.

'You look terrible,' Rose said as she studied his face.

'I feel terrible,' he replied.

'Did something happen today with Bradman? You were gone for an awful long time.'

Jim's head ached. He couldn't tell her. Couldn't say that he had murdered a man in cold blood. What would be his justification? Bradman had made him do it? As far as he could remember nobody else's finger but his own was on the trigger. No, Jim couldn't deal with this now. He was tired and confused and definitely needed some sleep.

'Everything's fine,' he reassured Rose, forcing a smile to his face. 'I'm just tired from all this work but it'll be worth it when I get to call you my wife. I just got to keep working to prove to your pa that I'm good enough for you.'

Rose smiled at him but she was a shrewd woman. She knew that there was something strange lurking behind Jim's forced smile but she decided not to press the matter. She was tired too and she bade Jim a good night.

Her sleep that night was fitful, however. A man's image kept recurring in her dreams but it wasn't Jim whom she saw. It was Mike Bradman. The man from the saloon whose eyes had never left her all night long. She woke with a start, sweat on her forehead. She fumbled for the candle at her side and lit up the room, half-afraid that Bradman was in the room with her, staring at her. She breathed a deep sigh of relief when she saw she was alone, those terrifying eyes weren't staring at her from the foot of her bed. She slept another couple of hours with the light on but it was an uncomfortable and restless sleep.

Jim had slept poorly also, the sound of the gunshot going off over and over again in his head, the sight of the blood pouring from the dead man filling his dreams. At the breakfast table Rose could see that Jim looked as tired as she.

'Who was that feller with the marshal?' she asked casually.

'I didn't like the look of him,' her father added. 'Cruel-looking face.'

'That's his brother, Mike,' said Jim.

'His brother!' Rose and her father exclaimed together.

'As if one of them isn't bad enough,' mumbled Rose.

'Now Rose,' her father said. 'Whatever about his brother, at least the marshal has started to do something about the lawlessness in this town. Isn't that right, Jim?'

Jim just grunted in reply but Rose's father was undeterred.

'Why, didn't you two catch them cattle rustlers yesterday? I heard there was a shoot-out and all.'

'Where'd you hear that?' Jim asked angrily.

Both Rose and her father looked at him in surprise. The fierceness in his voice had taken them aback.

'The marshal was talking about it last night,' Rose's father replied. 'Heard him say that you're a fast draw, Jim. That you pretty much saved his life by gunning that feller Baker down.'

'Baker!' Rose exclaimed. 'You killed Baker?'

Jim just looked into his cup of coffee.

'Baker was no cattle rustler. Hell, he was shot up himself already,' Rose continued.

'Now, Rose, you stop that. If the marshal says that Baker was the cattle rustler there must have been evidence. Even a lawman can't go around shooting people up without any evidence. Isn't that right, Jim?'

Jim just nodded, giving only a faint movement of his head. He felt empty and sick inside. He felt that he could taste Baker's blood in his mouth and he had difficulty swallowing his coffee.

'You spoke to me last night with blood on your hands!' she cried.

'The blood of a criminal, Rose,' her father interrupted, 'who was about to kill the marshal.'

'It was Baker, Pop,' she replied. 'Baker. He was a fool but nothing more. It was his brother who was the troublemaker.'

She turned to Jim. There was an icy look in her eyes that Jim had never seen before.

'But of course, he's dead because of you, too. Isn't he, Jim?'

Jim couldn't answer.

'Well I'll tell you both something.' Her voice was low, commanding attention even more than if she shouted the house down. 'I don't trust either of the Bradman brothers. They mean trouble, and if you keep on as Jake's deputy you'll never be able to call me your wife, Jim Boland. You've changed since you've started working with him, and not for the better.'

She stormed from the table leaving Jim and her father to sit in silence.

# 21

Jim was confused, unsure of what to do next. If he quit as deputy, as Rose would like him to do, he would have to find another job. He couldn't stick working in the saloon for long, that he knew for certain, even if Rose's father could afford to pay him. The liquor, the drunkenness, the violence: that wasn't Jim Boland. At least not any more. That just left cattle-herding. One thing he knew for certain, though, was that he couldn't leave Rose again. Going back on the trail was not an option. He'd have to stick with Jake for the time being, despite his misgivings and Rose's objections — he couldn't see any other way. He finished his breakfast and bade farewell to Cole.

*Never thought I'd see the day when I'd get on better with Rose's father than herself,* Jim thought.

Ellsworth was quiet as he strode down the street. The rail-heads were idle, the dance-halls, saloons, gambling dens and brothels all lay silent as Jim took in the morning air. He walked into Bradman's office and was relieved to see that Jake was by himself; there was no sign of his brother.

'Howdy,' Jim said. Jake sat slumped behind his desk.

'Howdy yourself,' Jake replied. His voice was hoarse from the drinking, smoking and shouting he had done last night.

His head was sore, a fiery tide sweeping through his brain. Every sound aggravated his sensitive nerve-endings and caused his mood to darken.

'Where's your brother?' Jim asked.

'Staying in a hotel.' With great effort Jake continued the conversation: 'You've got a sad looking face on you this morning,' he growled. 'That pretty little woman of yours giving you trouble?'

'She's not my pretty little woman,' Jim replied. 'We're not married.' He paused. 'Yet.'

'Well, I wouldn't wait around too long if I were you. A pretty little thing like that, in a town like this . . . ' The marshal left the rest unsaid but Jim knew exactly what he meant. He remembered Rose's objections earlier at breakfast and also his own distaste towards Bradman. Distaste made even more powerful now that his brother had joined him. But what choice did he have? He'd talk to Rose about it this evening. Today he would have to do his job as marshal's deputy in Ellsworth.

★　★　★

Mike Bradman opened his eyes and then quickly closed them again. It felt as if a Pacific Railroad loco was pounding through his head. He hadn't had an all out binge like last night for a long time. He'd needed it. He'd got a few things straightened out in his head now. Jake had set himself up pretty well here. Lawman. In the wickedest cow-town in the West, no less. He couldn't clean out the whole town but maybe he could get a cut of the business for himself and his brother. Mike smiled at the thought of Jake as a marshal. 'We'll run some cattle through this place and that's for sure,' he thought.

Costello, Mason and Lopez slept in the kitchen with the cold, hard floor poking into their backs. Their backs were stiff and their necks were sore and their moods weren't improved any further when they went through the cupboards and found them empty.

'A feller can't even have a cup of coffee in this place,' Costello complained.

'Big change from before,' Mason agreed.

'The boss knows what he's doing,' growled Lopez, growing angry with the other men's constant complaining. 'I'm sure he's got something planned. He always comes good, right?'

'I'm glad you have such faith in him,' came a voice from the doorway. It was Ella. She had slept in the spare bedroom. The night before, when she had heard Mike come back, steaming drunk, she had been worried. She had lain in the old, musty bed and pulled the blanket up to her chin. But Mike didn't look for her. He had just gone straight to bed. This was not all good news, however, Ella considered. It had spared her that which might have happened to her last night, but it also proved that Mike had grown tired of her. She knew now that her days were numbered. If it weren't to keep her as a plaything, she couldn't see why Mike would let her live. She would have to come up with a plan of escape. She knew that she wouldn't get any help from Lopez, Mike's loyal pup; or Mason, who was petrified of Mike. But Costello? Maybe. She would just have to see how things played out. She mustn't wait long, though. In this town of vice and whores it wouldn't be long before Mike had her replaced, for good.

There was a bang as the door swung open and Jake walked in.

'Howdy pardners,' he called, sounding more chirpy than he felt. His one good eye was red and he had a growth of stubble on his face as testament to the previous night's frivolities. The effects of the drink was beginning to wear off at last, however. And at least he had a full belly, having stopped for breakfast before leaving town.

'You bring anything to eat?' Costello spat.

'What a way to greet a guest,' Jake replied jokingly. Costello just glared at him. He hadn't had many dealings with the younger of the Bradman brothers and he was still wary of him. No matter who he was related to. If he was anything like Mike he would have a ruthless streak bred into him by a hard upbringing and as a result of having had to fight for everything he'd got. Legally or otherwise.

'Where's that brother of mine?' Jake asked.

Lopez pointed to the bedroom. 'Still sleeping it off.'

Jake laughed. 'Liquor always affected him more than me!' He pushed open the bedroom door and stepped inside. A blanket covered the window, preventing light from entering. He was met by a warm fug, a heavy heat mixed with the whiff of alcohol. Mike Bradman lay sprawled on the bed, he hadn't even made it under the covers.

'Morning, brother,' called Jake as he pulled the blanket from the window. The sun's rays penetrated into Mike's consciousness and roused him from his drunken sleep.

'What you doing here?' he croaked.

'Brought you some breakfast,' Jake replied.

'Get out and I'll be up in a minute.'

Jake returned to the kitchen. 'Never was a morning person,' he joked.

Ella had watched all the goings on from the safety of her room, as she had retreated in there when she saw Jake arrive. Her breath had caught when she had seen Jake enter and it seemed as if she had backed out of the kitchen instinctively, as if her legs were forcing her away from him. He looked just like

Mike, except with an eyepatch, of course. Jake saw her lingering in the doorway and sauntered towards her. A chill ran through her body and she shivered involuntarily.

'Well, well, well,' he said, his voice sweet as honey. 'This must be the beautiful Ella.' He stood in front of her, lust in his eyes. Even though she was just out of bed there was no disguising the shapeliness of her body beneath her cotton dress. She was a well-put-together lady, of that there could be no doubt. 'I can see why Mike decided to keep you, even after what happened.' He ran a finger through her hair. She flinched involuntarily, but still stood her ground.

'I don't know why he let her live,' Lopez said, viciously. 'If it was up to me she'd have been praying for death to come when I was finished with her.'

'Now, now, Hernan. I'm sure my brother has some plan for this little lady.' He reached down and grabbed her backside. This time Ella did react.

She grabbed his arm and pushed it away violently.

'Get your hands off me, you one-eyed donkey!' she hissed. She reached behind her for the door and tried to close it in his face. He stretched out his arm just in time to stop the door hitting him. He pushed firmly against it, opened it and shoved her back into the bedroom. He strode over to her and caught her roughly by the arm.

'What did you say,' he shouted. His voice had risen a pitch with anger.

'I said let go of me, you deformed monster!'

Jake raised his hand to hit her but it was stopped before it reached her face.

'Take it easy, Bradman,' soothed Costello. His voice had an edge too, however. Suggesting that there would be consequences if Jake didn't take too kindly to his request.

'Let go of my arm,' Jake hissed, his eyes burning into Costello's.

'No,' Costello replied firmly. 'Let go of her and let's all get some breakfast.

She's got a tongue like a rattlesnake but that don't mean that you can slap someone else's woman around.'

Jake glared at Costello. He wasn't used to having his authority questioned, certainly not since he became marshal of Ellsworth.

'She's my brother's woman,' he said through gritted teeth. 'And she tried to get him killed. I'm pretty sure he wouldn't mind if I taught her a few manners.'

Both men held their poses, neither willing to budge. Lopez and Mason didn't intervene. They both stood back, unsure of what course of action to take.

'What's going on?' came the rough, coarse voice of Mike Bradman. In all the commotion they hadn't noticed him emerge from his room. 'Jake? Costello? What you fellers doing?' Costello let go of Jake's hand. It dropped to his side and Ella took the opportunity to move out of his reach.

'I hope you fellers aren't fighting over Ella, here. She ain't worth the trouble.'

Mike sniggered. 'Ain't that right, Ella?' He moved towards her, swaying his hips suggestively. He cornered her against a wall. She could smell the drink on his breath and see the rheumy film in his eyes. He smelled of stale sweat, as well as dirt and grime. How had she once been so charmed by this creature? He pushed his face close against hers, his stubble hurting her skin.

'Don't get too close to her, though, boys. Or you might get a nasty surprise, as I found out!' He laughed at his own joke and turned away from her. She relaxed her shoulders and body like a cat after a dog decides it's not so hungry after all.

'Make us some breakfast, Ella. And try to make it edible. At least make yourself someway useful around here.'

Ella did as she was told; she knew her survival depended on it but as she cooked she occasionally stole a glance at Costello and wondered what his motives were for saving her from a beating.

# 22

Jim spent the day around Ellsworth following up on complaints of routine violence and robbery. Harry was on his mind as well. He still showed no real signs of recovery and Jim knew that if he didn't regain consciousness soon . . . Well, it didn't bear thinking about. Thoughts of Rose weighed heavily on his mind, too. Thoughts of their future together, if they had one. He thought about how just as he seemed to have won Rose's father over, she picked a fight with him.

He shook his head, wearily. The only reason he was staying in Ellsworth was for her. The only way he could stay in Ellsworth was if he could earn his own money, have a steady job. But now Rose was saying that she might not marry him if he kept that job. His head hurt with all these thoughts. But one inescapable truth remained — he agreed with Rose in regard to Jake Bradman. He didn't trust him either. The only question was what was he going to do about it?

★ ★ ★

Back at the old Baker homestead, the plot's new inhabitants were just finishing their breakfast.

'Not too bad,' Mike said patronizingly. 'Maybe I'll keep you on as a cook.' Ella cleared the table of plates and went outside to wash them. Jake took the opportunity to talk to Mike about her.

'What's going on?' he asked. 'You shouldn't hold on to a dog that bites, brother.'

'I know,' Mike replied. His hunger had eased and the coffee had helped clear his mind and improve his mood. 'She'll pay for what she did, don't any of you worry.' He spoke slowly and deliberately looking around the table as he did so. 'Right now, she'll be useful around the house here until we get up and running. After that? We'll see.'

Ella returned and the topic of conversation changed.

'What's the plan?' Lopez asked Mike. 'Rustle some cattle, make some money?' A smile creased his face. 'Have some fun?'

'Something like that,' Mike replied. 'But this could be even better than before. With Jake as marshal we can't go wrong. No matter what we do we've got the law on our side. Isn't that right, brother?'

'Damn right!' Jake replied and they dashed their coffee mugs together.

'We can hit the gamblers,' Mike continued, 'the women, the traders, the cattlemen, the farmers. We're now in control of the town of Ellsworth. It just doesn't know it yet!'

★ ★ ★

Later that evening Jim sat at the table eating his supper, in exactly the same spot where Rose had argued with him that morning. This time he sat alone, however, deep in thought. Cole was in the saloon keeping one eye on the early-evening trade. Jim was so wrapped up in his concerns that he didn't notice Rose entering the room.

'Jim,' she said softly as she laid her hand on his shoulder. 'I'm sorry about this morning.' He put down his knife and fork and stared up into her face. He loved that face, that girl, of that there was no doubt. And he would do anything to please her.

'I'm sorry, too,' he began. Rose cut him off with a shake of her head. 'You've nothing to apologize for,' she replied. 'It was me that nearly bit your head off. You know what I can be like.' She sat on the seat next to Jim and rested her head on his shoulder. He ran his fingers through her curly red hair. They had never been so close, Jim thought, but there was still something separating them.

Rose continued speaking. 'I'm hot headed. I talk first and think later. I fell for you the second I saw you, Jim

Boland, but in the same way I was wary of Bradman when I first saw him. It wasn't the eye-patch or the scar. There was more to it. Know what I mean?' She didn't give Jim time to answer. She continued: 'You just do what you have to do to stay here in Ellsworth, Jim, I really mean that.'

He stared into her earnest face. She loved him, of that he was certain. Why else would she be lying to him.

'No, you don't, Rose,' Jim replied. He stared hard at her. She began to reply but stopped herself. 'I think that maybe you could convince yourself that you could marry me. That what I did for a living didn't matter. But one day you'd come to realize that it does matter. You're a principled gal, Rose, and you wouldn't stay with a feller that was doing what you felt was wrong.'

'No, Jim,' she protested. 'That's not true.'

'There's no need to speak,' Jim continued. 'I think I agree with your gut feeling, anyway. I'm not sure that I can keep on working with Jake. He's as big a crook as anybody in this town as far as I can see. And dangerous too.'

Rose's heart skipped a beat. 'But what are you going to do, Jim? I don't want you back on the trail. Maybe Daddy can fix you up with a job here?'

'Maybe,' Jim agreed. 'But I'm not sure he can afford to take on a feller like me. I'm not as quick behind the bar as the rest of you and my temper wouldn't last long with them drunk jiggers if I had to face them every night.'

'But what then?' Rose pleaded.

'I don't know,' Jim replied slowly. 'All I know is cattle. That's what it keeps coming down to.'

'So you'd leave me again?' Rose was indignant now. She felt that Jim was giving up too easily, too eager to leave town and return to the trail. 'I think you love them cattle more than you love me. If you don't want to marry me, Jim Boland, just say so. That's what a man would do, at least!' She rose to go but Jim grabbed her arm. It felt good to the touch, soft between his fingers.

'That's not the case. But you know how hard it is for an outsider to find work in this town.'

She just glared at him. 'Fine,' she said at last. 'How's about we reach a compromise? You keep working with that jigger Bradman for the time being but keep your eyes open for another job. How's about that?'

'If that's what it takes to stay here with you, it's worth it. I can do my best to stay out of his way.'

'Talk to people, Jim,' Rose went on. 'They'll see you're a nice feller. You'll get another job here in town if you try hard enough. How about the cattle-yard? Have you thought of that?'

Jim had to admit that he hadn't.

'Now stop feeling sorry for yourself and go get dressed!'

Jim looked puzzled. 'But I am dressed.'

'In your fancy clothes, idiot!'

'For what?'

'Pop gave me the night off, we're going to the dance!'

# 23

The diversion was exactly what Jim needed. He dressed in his fanciest clothes and felt mighty proud walking through the doors of the Grand Central Hotel with the prettiest lady in town on his arm. As they entered they were greeted with the upbeat tunes played by the musicians on their fiddles and the warm fug of cigarette smoke and body heat. The room was filled with people talking, drinking and dancing and the sound of men and women talking complemented the stamping of boots of the wooden floor. Sometimes in time with the music, but mostly not.

They danced and laughed and lost themselves in the enjoyment of the night. When Jim Boland awoke the next morning he felt as if the pall that had hung over him for the last few days had lifted. He had a plan with which to move forward. Now he just had to go through with it. What he didn't know as he rose that morning was that there had been trouble out on the trail during the night.

★ ★ ★

Two men were waiting for Jim when he entered the marshal's office. 'Cal Mitchell,' he whispered. 'It's been a long time.' Dan Mitchell's son looked as surprised as Jim.

'So, the rumours are true. You really are deputy here,' he replied. Jim just nodded. 'You know something,' Cal continued, 'I think your father would be pretty proud of you if he saw you now, Jim. And your ma, too. You've made something of yourself. That's all a feller can ask for.'

Jim just nodded his silent thanks for Cal's kind words. Cal introduced his companion as Winfield, the trail boss of a company of drovers bringing cattle to Ellsworth. Cal was working as his ramrod. They both looked in rough shape. At first, Jim thought that they had been in a brawl in some bar or had been robbed in a honky-tonk, but he soon found out that something far more sinister was afoot. They explained to the two lawmen that they had been herding about 3,000 head of cattle towards Ellsworth when they had settled for the night outside the town.

'What happened then?' Jim asked.

'These jiggers came along and stampeded the cattle. We lost over half of them. The rest of the fellers are at the railyard now with the remainder of the cattle. We came up here just now to tell you fellers about it. See if you could help us out.'

'We haven't had much problems with rustlers. At least, not since I've been marshal. Ain't that right, Jim?' Jim put the thought of the rustling accusations against Baker out of his mind. He knew Jake was taking a swing at him but he chose to ignore it.

'That's right, Jake. We haven't had

rustlers around here for a while.' The room fell silent until Jim continued: 'How many of them were there?'

'Not rightly sure,' Winfield replied. He was obviously still shaken, his face as white as a sheet. 'They knocked out the two night guards and stampeded the cattle. We could have all been killed.'

'When did you figure out that some of the cattle were missing.'

'Well, we rode hard after them and eventually turned them. We knew right away that there were some missing but we figured that we had lost them in the stampede.'

'That was until we saw the tracks,' Mitchell intervened.

'What tracks?' asked Jake. He sounded edgy, Jim thought. But, then again, who knew what went on in Jake Bradman's head?

'When we got the cattle back to the bedding ground we saw tracks leading away towards Ellsworth.'

'What kind of tracks?' Jim asked.

'Animal or human?'

'Both. Horses, cattle and men. As if they had taken away as many cattle as they could manage and stampeded the rest.'

'Why would they have taken only some of the herd?' Jake asked. 'Why not take it all? That makes no sense.'

'I don't know,' Winfield replied. 'Me and Cal were just talking about that. We figured that there must only have been a few of the jiggers. They most likely couldn't manage a whole herd so they took what they could and scattered the rest to buy some time.'

'Do you think they took them to the railhead?'

'That's what we're here for, fellers. You're the law, you know the place better than us. What do you think these jiggers would have done?' Cal and Winfield were getting agitated now, thinking that there were too many questions and not enough action. Jim, seeing that Jake wasn't going to speak, reassured the two drovers that they would do everything they could to get the cattle back.

After the two men had left Jake turned to Jim. 'You know that feller?' he asked about Cal.

'From a long time ago,' Jim replied. 'From a different life.'

'What did he mean about your father being proud? He dead or something?'

Jim's face fell; memories that he had buried were being dredged up again. A still silence filled the room.

Jim broke through the uncomfortable pause by asking Jake whether he should check out the railyards. 'Why not?' Jake shrugged. He seemed distracted and turned his face away from Jim. 'I don't know if it'll do any good, though.'

'What d'you mean?' Jim asked, a little suspicious.

'Nothing,' Jake answered quickly. 'I don't mean nothing. Check out the railyards and let me know how you get on. See you later.' Jake gathered up his gear and left the room quickly.

Jim followed him out and watched

him mount up. He waited a few moments before hopping up on Jesse. He didn't head for the railyard, however, but followed Jake from a distance. Jake travelled slowly along Main Street, occasionally tipping his hat to the early-morning pedestrians. He certainly knew how to work the crowd, Jim thought. To all and sundry it appeared that he was doing a good job, keeping the citizens safe. But Jim knew otherwise. Or did he? What proof did he have, after all? If he levelled any accusation against Bradman all the marshal would have to do was point out that Jim had killed an unarmed man. Who's word would the people trust? Jake Bradman, town marshal. Or Jim Boland? Drunkard, troublemaker, out-sider.

Jim knew the answer to that particu-lar question.

# 24

He rode on, keeping a safe distance behind Bradman. It was easy to stay hidden while they were in the town but as the buildings thinned out and the land opened up ahead trailing Bradman would become more difficult. He hung back, stopping Jesse from going into a canter as they left the town behind. Jesse wasn't too happy with the restraint, eager instead to be off and running across the open fields. Jim held him strong, however, falling far enough back to be able just to see Bradman disappearing over the brow of a hill up ahead.

The trail led across flat farmland once over the hill. Jim stopped just shy of the peak and dismounted. He strode up to the top and lay down on his belly. He saw Bradman plodding on ahead, a good distance ahead, now. He veered to his right, off the trail. He didn't seem to think that there was anyone following him as he didn't look around once. He seemed preoccupied, Jim thought.

Something must have spiked his resolve, though, as all of a sudden he dug his heels into his horse's flank. The animal skittered sideways for a moment before surging forward. Jim didn't need to speed after him. He knew where he was going. There was only one homestead out in that direction. Baker's.

This development could not be good but Jim had to find out what was going on out there for certain. He rode more quickly now, letting Jesse stretch his legs. There was no worry that he might run into Bradman, certainly not at the pace at which he had taken off and the gap that had been between them. The trail took him across good farmland, land that the Baker brothers had worked. They were isolated out here, always had been and that was the way they liked it. Close enough to town but yet far enough away as well. Unfortunately, that had also marked them out as an easy target for Bradman.

The Baker homestead stood alone in a small valley. Jim slowed Jesse as he crested the hillock that overlooked the house and gradually drew him to a stop.

'This is close enough, buddy. Don't want to be rushing into something we can't get out of,' he mumbled.

Jim instinctively made for a small copse of trees to give him some cover. Even though he was still a fair distance from the house, the crisp morning air and the clear sky helped him get a good view of what lay below him. And he didn't particularly like what he saw. Jake's horse grazed in front of the house but there were also four others fenced in to a paddock by the side of the building. Baker's house was obviously not uninhabited, as it was supposed to be. But there was an altogether more disturbing sight in the grassland nearby. Cattle grazed peacefully, roaming around the field. Jim knew one thing for certain, that if he checked the branding on them they would match the half-herd that had been driven into Ellsworth by Winfield and Cal the day before.

★ ★ ★

The door to the wooden house burst open. Lopez automatically cocked his gun and aimed at the figure that filled the doorway.

'You fools!' spat the figure in the doorway, 'what have you done?'

'Jeez, take it easy, Jake,' Lopez said in reply. He eased the hammer of his revolver back into place, 'you almost got yourself a new talk-hole.'

Jake slammed the door behind him and stormed into the room. It was a sore and sorry sight that greeted him. All inside seemed the worse for wear.

'Brother, what's eating at you?' Mike asked.

'You know well what's eating at me. You fellers go off on a raid and don't even tell me? That wasn't how we agreed to do things.'

'I didn't realize that I had to run everything by you. Heck, I've to go to the latrine now, if that's OK with you. You like that? That what you want? Us to come running to you every time we want to do something?'

The hard edge in Mike's voice caught Jake by surprise. He had been full of anger when he had ridden out there, ready to lay down the law and assert his authority. This was his town, they'd have to play by his rules. For once, Jake and not big brother Mike would be calling the shots. It didn't seem to be panning out that way, however.

'I run my outfit the way I like,' Mike continued. He moved towards Jake, closing the distance between them quickly. 'And you, like everyone else, will get your cut, provided you do your bit properly. OK?'

Jake glared at him. The two men were just inches from each other. Two big, powerful figures, stubborn and strong.

One was going to have to give way. It was Jake.

'All right,' he mumbled.

'Good,' Mike replied. He held Jake's gaze until the younger brother turned his eyes away, the sign of submission that Mike was waiting for. 'Now, I've got to go outside like I said, and I ain't asking anyone's permission.'

Jim saw the figure emerge from the house. At first he thought it was Jake but he quickly realized that this man had no eye-patch. 'Mike,' he whispered in surprise. 'So you fellers ain't staying in no hotel.' His suspicions had been confirmed. It looked as though the Bradman brothers were up to no good. He waited for Mike to finish his business and go back into the house. As soon as the door closed he eased Jesse around, preparing to ride back to town. Something stopped him, though: a movement from the corner of his eye. He swung Jesse round again so that he could get a full view of the area below. Nothing. He must have imagined it.

But then he saw it again, a figure dashing away from the house with her head down, obviously trying to stay hidden from those inside, limping as she ran.

*Just what the hell is going on in that house?* he wondered.

★ ★ ★

Ella had heard the door bang and Jake shouting. She had been lying on the bed in her room, with the door open so that Mike could keep an eye on her. It had been a long night. When they had left on their raid she had seriously thought about trying to escape. But Mike had kept one step ahead of her, and had tied one of her hands and one of her legs to the bed before he left. It had made her more determined to get away, however. He didn't trust her. Fair enough. But for how long would he go to the bother of tying her up rather than just putting a bullet in her? That was a question she couldn't answer.

When they had returned, just before first light, they had been delirious. They had rustled up some bottles of whiskey from somewhere and had drunk until now. Were still drinking in fact. Mike had come into her room and untied her, and made some suggestive comments about what he would do to her later. Thankfully, later had never come and Mike had just continued on drinking.

When Jake had burst through the front door, Ella had taken her chance and closed the door to her room, Mike and the others had been distracted, with any luck they would remain so. She slipped through the makeshift curtain and out of the window, keeping hunched over to avoid being seen. Her heart beat wildly, as if it were trying to burst from her chest and her injured ankle slowed her down. She didn't know where she was going, or where she was going to find help. But, as long as she was away from Mike Bradman, she'd take her chances.

Glancing up, she saw the small copse of trees ahead. She had thought of the best way to escape when she had been outside washing the dishes and drawing water from the well, but as she didn't know which way the town lay she had decided that the trees would provide her with some cover. At least to begin with. The plan then was to get to the rim of the bowl in which the cottage was situated and see how the land lay from there. Not much of a plan, but better than nothing.

She ran as fast as she could, no longer bent over but pumping her arms and legs, her dress flowing out behind her, doing her best to ignore the stabbing pain in her ankle. Her breath was shallow, exhaled in short bursts, the strain of the sprint pressuring her lungs. She drew closer to the trees. Then she heard the first shot and felt the zip of a bullet as it passed her by. She didn't look back but kept running. Straight towards where Jim was hiding.

# 25

Jim sat on Jesse, bemused and confused by what he was watching. The woman covered the ground quickly, drawing closer to him with every stride. He thought about breaking cover and riding out to meet her but something held him back. But then he saw the door to the house open again, and he knew something bad was about to happen. A man stood framed in the doorway; it wasn't either of the Bradmans, of that he was sure, his pistol was drawn. He heard the report from the gun, and knew the target was the escaping woman. The bullet missed her and thudded into a tree near to Jim's head. Too close for comfort. The man fired again and a clump of dust rose at the woman's feet. The shooter was getting closer.

*Damn it, Jim, you can't stay out of*

*trouble. Can you?* he thought.

He made his mind up fast. He spurred Jesse forward into the open. The woman was only yards from him now. Another report. Jim felt a sharp pain across the top of his head. His hand shot up. His hat was gone and he felt blood. He held on to Jesse's reins, his knuckles white. He drew his own revolver and fired two shots quickly at the shooter. He shot wildly but he hoped the sound of the gun, if not the accuracy of the shots might buy him some time.

Lopez took cover. He didn't know who was shooting at him or where the lead had ended up but he sure didn't feel like getting his head shot off, so he dove back inside and closed the door. Mike and Mason had found their guns and were about to join him.

'You get her?' Mike spat.

'Nope. There's some jigger out there with her, firing back.'

Unseen, Costello allowed himself a smile.

236

'What?' Mike was furious, his face florid with temper. 'Come on,' he said to his men.

Two more bullets bit into the wooden walls of the house, keeping them inside. Mike led the way towards his bedroom. This room was at the back of the house, allowing them to slip out through the window in safety. They had their weapons drawn as they crept around the side of the house, ready to fire. On Mike's signal they fanned out and unloaded a volley of shots up the valley. There was no one there; all that remained of Ella and the mysterious rider was his Stetson lying in the dust.

★　★　★

Ella gripped tightly on to Jim as they rode away from the Baker homestead. She didn't know this man, had never seen him before, but he had saved her life. That was an improvement on her situation with Mike, at least. She could see blood flowing from a wound on the top of his head but it didn't seem to be slowing him down. They rode hard and fast, away from the scene of the shoot-out. She closed her eyes and let her head fall on to Jim's back, smelling the sweat through his shirt. She was exhausted, both mentally and physically. She would rest now, at least until they got to their destination.

Jim rode into town and round the back of Rose's father's saloon. He slid off Jesse and helped Ella down. In truth, she pretty much fell off and he caught her as she dropped. They hadn't spoken to each other, hadn't shared a word. But now was not the time. They had to get under cover, away from prying eyes. He didn't know whether he had been recognized back at the farm. He didn't think he had, at least he hoped he hadn't; he had kept low as he fired, and believed he had been far enough away from the house to escape recognition. No matter, this was the only place in town he could go, anyway. He supported Ella as they walked in through the back door. Who was this mysterious woman? What must she be running from? The questions didn't bear too much contemplation. She'd been holed up in that house with Mike Bradman, and obviously a few more besides. All he knew was that it was no place for a woman. Certainly not for one as attractive as this.

Rose turned as the back door opened and the two figures staggered into the kitchen. It took her a moment to recognize Jim. Blood, mixed with dry dust, covered half his face. She looked at the woman he carried and stared open-mouthed. She saw that they were both weak; the woman looked as if she were about to collapse and Jim wasn't much better. She spun two chairs around to face them and ran over to help Jim. She supported the woman's other shoulder as they stumbled across the kitchen floor. The woman slumped into a chair, her chin lolling on to her chest. She had passed out. Jim collapsed into another. He looked terrible, half-dead.

'Jim?' Rose's voice sounded tiny, terror and worry constricting her throat.

'Just a flesh wound,' he replied. 'Water, please.'

★ ★ ★

Mike picked up the Stetson and held it to the sun. the bullet hole was clearly visible, the sunlight shining through the hole in the fabric. Blood stained the ground, also.

'He's hurt, he should be easy to spot,' Mike said.

'I don't know,' Jake replied. 'There are a lot of shot-up jiggers in Ellsworth.'

Mike just nodded, he knew that his brother was right. 'If we ride out now, we might catch them,' he said grimly. They all turned to go back to the house, all except Jake.

'There's no need,' he said. 'I know where we'll find her.'

They looked at him expectantly. 'This is Boland's 'Boss of the Plains' hat, I've been looking at it on his thick head for the past week.'

Mike allowed himself a smile. 'Well, let's get going. What are we waiting for?'

Jake challenged him, however. 'No, Mike. This time we do it my way.'

The four men had turned away from Jake and had been making their way towards their horses. Now, after hearing him speak, they paused. Costello looked at Mike out of the corner of his eye, unsure of how he was going to react to his brother's challenge.

Mike wasn't used to being questioned, and he usually reacted badly when when he was.

Jake saw Mike turn to face him, his face like thunder. The others turned, too, but only Lopez looked as angry as Mike. Costello and Mason just looked uneasy and, Jake noted, they were keeping their hands hovering over their holsters.

'What did you just say?' Mike spat.

'You heard me.' Jake's voice was

strong. If he felt nervous, his words weren't betraying him. Mike strode towards his brother, every one of his muscles tensed.

'You better keep your mouth shut, little brother, or I'm going to have to shut it for you. Nobody tells me what to do.' Mike's voice was low, his face contorted as if he were forcing each word out through clenched teeth. 'I don't want to embarrass you, Jake,' he continued. His voice dripped with menace. He looked like a spring, tightly coiled and ready to explode.

'This is my town, Mike. You're not going shooting it up. You fellers already caused enough trouble last night with your raid. If you'd come to me first we could have managed it a lot better. This isn't like some hick town that you might have run before, Mike. This is Ellsworth. A goldmine if we do things properly.'

'You mean if we do things your way?'

Jake paused before replying. Surely Mike couldn't be coming around to his way of thinking? 'Yes.'

Mike's right arm flashed forward, his fist connecting neatly with Jake's chin. Jake fell to the ground, caught cold by the punch. The first thing that made him realize that he had been hit was his head bouncing off the dusty ground. A shooting pain crossed his lower face. Mike was on him, glaring in his face, gun drawn. He cocked the hammer and pressed the cold steel barrel hard against Jake's cheek. Jake felt as if his face was going to be pushed into the ground, the pressure of the barrel and the pain from the punch made him want to cry out. But somehow he held himself together. He stared into Mike's face, mesmerized by the murderous look in his eyes.

'Don't you ever question me again!' Mike screamed. He lowered his face even more, their heads were almost touching, Mike's head blocking out Jake's vision so that all he could see was his manic expression. Mike's face was red from fury and frustration. Spit flecked from his mouth and landed on Jake's cheek.

Jake couldn't muster his wits in order to reply to Mike. The ferocity of his brother's attack had overwhelmed him.

'Be careful, brother,' Mike hissed. 'Or I might finish the job I started the last time.' He traced a line from Jake's eye-patch down the scar on his cheek with the barrel of the gun, pushing hard at the end, jamming Jake's face once more into the dust. Then he rose to his feet and looked intently at the others, challenging them to question his authority. Unsurprisingly, none did.

'Lopez, Mason,' he barked. The two men jumped to attention. 'Stay here with the cattle.' They nodded. 'Costello, come with me.'

'To get Ella?' Costello asked.

Mike nodded. 'You,' he shouted back to Jake. 'Stop wallowing in the dust and come with us. You know the town the best.' Jake had no choice but to do what he was told. Mike was in charge and that was the beginning and the end of it.

# 26

Rose bathed Jim's face. They had put Ella on to Rose's bed. She had merely mumbled a few times as Jim had lifted her in. She was out cold, dead to the world. The basin of water in front of Rose was a dull red from the wound on Jim's scalp.

'Scalp wounds bleed a lot,' Jim had told her, 'but they're generally not too dangerous.'

'I'd say that any day that you get hit by a bullet is a dangerous one,' Rose had replied. Her concern was obvious on her face. When she had seen Jim come through the door she thought he was about to drop down dead. He had looked as if half of his face had been blown away. At least now, as she sponged away the dried blood, she could see the actual wound. It was a small nick, a graze above his right temple. A glancing blow from the bullet, but a bullet wound nonetheless.

Now that she knew that Jim wasn't in danger of dying in her kitchen she felt that she could ask him all about this crazy situation. In particular about how he had been shot and by whom. And, most important, who was the undeniably beautiful woman he had been carrying. Even though she knew that she was being ridiculous, Rose had felt a pang of jealousy when she saw Jim tenderly carry that woman into the house and into her bedroom: a jealousy that she now hid behind a stern tone.

'What the heck have you been up to, Jim? And who in heaven's name is that woman?'

Jim told her the story in full, including the encounters with the drovers in the marshal's office that morning.

'Do Jake and Mike know that it was you who rescued her?' Rose asked.

'I don't think so,' Jim replied. 'I kept hidden as best I could, and they were a long ways back.'

'Who do you think she is?'

Jim paused before answering, working through ideas in his head. 'I'm not sure,' he said, at last. 'But I figure if she's running from the Bradman brothers we've got to help her.'

Rose nodded in agreement. She was pale, her face as white as chalk. 'You look like you've seen a ghost,' Jim said gently.

'I thought I was seeing a dead man when you came through that door,' she replied.

He smiled at her and jostled her shoulder affectionately. 'It's just a graze. Take more than that to kill me.'

Tears welled up in her eyes. She had almost lost him. Even in this wild town where people were hurt or killed almost daily, she had never cared about anyone so much that she feared so for their life, except maybe her father and late mother.

Jim reached out and grabbed her, drawing her close. He hugged her tight.

'I'm here,' he said. 'I'm not going anywhere.'

The tears fell silently from her eyes. She let him hold her. They stayed like that for what seemed like for ever, but still not long enough: an embrace like a cocoon that shielded them from the rest of the world.

Until a voice from behind startled them. 'Where am I?' asked Ella.

Rose and Jim broke their embrace and turned to face her. 'You're safe,' Jim said, 'that's the most important thing. But before we get too familiar, you better answer a few of our questions.'

Ella wavered, staggering a little on unsteady feet. Jim rose and gave her his chair.

'Some coffee, Rose,' he said. Rose went to the stove and heated some water as Jim stood over Ella. Neither Jim nor Rose noticed that she covertly checked out the room, the way out and anything that could be used as a weapon. Her survival instincts were kicking back in.

Jim's wound had started bleeding once more and a small trickle of bright-red blood ran down his forehead.

'You were hit,' Ella said.

'Just a graze.' Jim waved his hand, dismissive of his injury. 'Anyway, that's not important. Who exactly are you, and why are you running from the Bradman brothers? That's what's important.'

Ella remained quiet. Rose finished brewing the coffee and placed the mug on the table in front of Ella. She took a few small sips from it, liquid slowly bringing her back to life.

'We've got to do some trading here,' she said. 'You give me something, I give you something.' Jim glanced at Rose.

'Fine,' Rose said. 'You're in a saloon in Ellsworth and you're safe. That's all you need to know until you tell us who you are and what's going on. Jim got shot because of you, so unless you want to be handed back to the Bradmans you'd better start talking.'

Ella was in a bind, that much was obvious, but at least she was no longer at Mike's mercy. She decided to talk. She told them everything, and when she had finished both Jim and Rose stared at her open-mouthed. It was an amazing story, and one that crystallized in Jim's mind the danger posed by the Bradman brothers.

★ ★ ★

They rode out from the Baker homestead, destruction on their minds. Jake led the way, followed behind by Mike and Costello. Jake could feel his brother's eyes burning into his back. He was tense and also embarrassed. The humiliation he had suffered at Mike's hands only served to stoke the flames of his temper. That wasn't the first time that his brother had beaten him down. But it had been the first time for a long time. Since . . . His hand instinctively touched his eye-patch, the outward sign of the incident that had shaped his life.

And it would be the last time Mike laid a hand on him, he vowed. A plan hatched in his head that would rid him of all his annoyances for once and for all.

The streets of Ellsworth had grown busy by the time the horsemen drew near. Cattle were being driven towards the stockyard and businesses were benefiting from the drovers. The season was coming to a close and both the visitors and the natives were determined to get the most from the dying embers of another cattle-year. The four horsemen blended with the crowds as they headed for the Southern Belle. Costello's hands gripped his horse's reins tightly as they drew closer, anxiety and uncertainty coursing through him. Just as they drew close Mike bawled out an order.

'Wait!' he shouted. Jake, Mason and Costello drew next to him. 'You,' he pointed at Jake. 'Go see if that horse of his is tethered out back.' Jake dismounted and made his way carefully round the side of the saloon to the stables. Sure enough, there Jesse was, drinking heartily from a bucket of water. Jake returned to Mike and passed on the information. 'They're in there,' Jake said. 'He never goes anywhere without that horse.'

Mike paused a moment, thinking. 'Let's wait until later, then, going in after her now might only draw too much attention. Blow our cover for good. We'll come back tonight, when the saloon's busy. Go in the back and be gone before anyone knows what's happening. And if anyone does hear anything it'll be lost in the chaos. Those jiggers'll be so drunk they'll start shooting at each other given half a chance.'

'So, what'll we do now?' Costello asked. 'Head back?'

'Nope,' Mike replied. 'The stockyard. Let's see if we can get rid of them cattle somehow and make a little money.' Costello dug his heels into his mount's side to get him moving. 'Not you, though,' Mike called to him. 'You stay here and keep an eye out. If she appears, you get her. Bring her back to the house. Otherwise, we'll see you tonight.'

Mike, Mason and Jake rode away towards the stockyard. In a way, Costello was relieved that they weren't trying to recapture Ella now. He still wasn't sure of his feelings towards her or whether he would fight for her if the situation demanded. On the other hand, a new danger had reared its head. If they were waiting until tonight to go to the saloon then Mike had no intention of letting Ella leave alive.

Jake thought about going back and warning Jim, just to spite Mike, but he could feel his brother's eyes on him. Watching him, waiting for him to do something stupid. What good would it do anyway? Instead, he finalized the plan he had been thinking of earlier. A plan that would mean that tonight would be the last night above ground for both Mike and Jim. He smiled at that thought. The smile then turned to a leer as he thought of Rose and Ella, alone, without their protectors. For now, he would have to play along with Mike, but not for much longer. His time would come. He was going to make sure of it.

★ ★ ★

'They'll find me, you know,' Ella said. There was no fear in her voice, just certainty. As if she was full sure that Mike would track her down.

'Why do you think that? Maybe they'll let you go?' Rose asked.

'I know too much. I know everything about them. And . . . ' Here she paused, 'Mike feels that he owns me. You don't understand.' She looked close to tears, the first sign of any real emotion since she had been carried in by Jim. 'He'll keep after me until either I'm dead, or he is.'

'Well, there's only one way to resolve that problem,' Jim muttered.

Rose glared at him. 'Can I talk with you for a minute, Jim? Alone?' She glanced towards Ella who took the hint. She left the kitchen and returned to the bedroom.

'What exactly are you thinking, Jim Boland? Sometimes you're as easy to read as an angry bull, but I have to admit that I haven't a clue as to what's going on in that head of yours right now.'

Jim smiled. 'That makes two of us. I'm not entirely sure of what I'm going to do either, but as far as I can see I have to do something. It's like this. Jake Bradman is a corrupt, dangerous man and he'll run the town into the ground if he remains as marshal. His brother, Mike, is also a very dangerous man and a cattle rustler, if we believe Ella. And I do believe her after my experiences out at the Baker place. As far as I can see, we have to take these two fellers out of the picture if we're to ever have a life together here, Rose. And I guess we'll have to deal with Mike's gang too.'

'How're you going to do that?' Rose

asked, not really sure whether she wanted to hear the answer.

'I'm not sure. It seems to be just me against the Bradman gang. I can't imagine that I'd get much support to go against the marshal. Not yet anyway. He hasn't burned enough bridges yet. I'll just have to take my chances and see what happens.'

'Maybe not.' The voice was Ella's. she had crept back to the kitchen door to listen to what was being said. She had been worried that Rose would try to persuade Jim to put her back on the street, convince him that she was too dangerous to have around. But on hearing how Jim spoke she knew that he had spoken the truth. That the only way that she, too, could be free was to face down Mike. She would have to help Jim any way she could, and she had an idea. And it involved Costello.

Looking out of her window she had seen him wandering around. At first she had drawn back, afraid that Mike would be with him but she quickly deduced that he was alone. It was this aloneness that she planned to exploit. She outlined her plan quickly to Jim and Rose. They would have to act fast, in case Mike returned.

★　★　★

Costello had watched Mike, Mason and Jake disappear down the street towards the stockyard. As soon as they had vanished from sight he made his way down the side of the saloon. The ground was packed hard and the soles of his boots made a noise as he walked along. He kept his hands on his holster, just in case. In truth, he had no great plan, no fantastic scheme. All he knew was that he didn't want Ella to be lying in a pool of blood that evening. She reminded him of the life he had left behind. He had had a family, a wife. But the war had changed everything. Once he had seen what he'd seen, done what he'd done, he knew he could never go back to them. That was why he had gone with Mike Bradman. The stealing, killing, intimidating; he could do it easily, without thinking. And if he didn't think, he didn't remember. Didn't remember Marie and what might have become of her. He could never go back to her again.

She had remarried, assuming that he was dead. He had visited his home, since the war had ended. She was happy, he knew that as he looked in the windows of their old house that night. His returning could only ruin things for her. And, anyway, it wouldn't be the man she had married who would be returning, but a used-up shell, bitter and violent. A product of his warlike environment. Better to leave things be. To never want a better life.

But then there was Ella. He had only recently begun to spend more time around her, having gained Mike's trust. A trust that he had previously bestown only upon Hernan Lopez. She had charmed Costello, but she probably didn't even realize it, he reasoned. She gave him the vision of an 'other'. Something that he had thought he had left behind, a way out from the trancelike state of constant death and destruction that had swallowed him up. Now, he had to think fast and make a decision, something he hadn't had to do for a very long time.

He lurked in the shadows, watching the back of the saloon. There was no sign of activity, no evidence that Ella was around. That was until she opened the door. His breath caught. What should he do? She took the decision out of his hands, however, and beckoned him towards her.

She looked furtively around, panic in her eyes as he approached her. Maybe she had been wrong, she wondered. Maybe it was a trap.

Costello's words calmed her: 'Its all right. I'm alone.' He crossed the back street quickly and passed through the door where he was promptly greeted by the business end of Jim's revolver and

Rose's Winchester. Ella banged the door behind him. He was the one who had been trapped.

'Drop your gun,' Jim said. Costello sized up the situation. There was no way that he could outdraw this much firepower. He loosened his gunbelt and let it drop to the ground. 'You know something?' he said, glancing up at Ella. 'Mike was right. You are a dangerous woman. Can't be trusted.' He had been foolish, his heart felt as if it were being crushed in a vice.

Jim stepped forward and kicked Costello's guns away from him, out of his reach.

'Sit down.'

Costello did as he was ordered. He sat heavily in the wooden chair, a defeated look on his face. 'What're you jiggers going to do? Shoot me? You might as well. Mike's going to kill me anyway if he finds me here.'

Jim opened his mouth to speak but Ella cut across him. 'We don't want to shoot you.'

Costello looked at her closely. 'You don't know what you're doing. Everyone who gets near you gets hurt. One way or another. You mightn't be the one pulling the trigger but somebody always ends up with a bullet in them.' The hurt in his voice was there for all to hear. Jim mentally gave Ella some credit. She knew how to read men right enough. She had told them that Costello had feelings for her, and it seemed that she was right, the pain in his eyes told them so. Now, Jim wondered, could she repair the damage done by this surprise gun-party and bend him to her will?

'Lee,' she said softly to Costello. She waved to Jim and Rose to lower their guns. 'We're not going to hurt you.' She crossed the floor to him until she stood over him. She lifted the hat from his head and ran her hand through his hair. Rose and Jim shared a look. Costello tried to keep his gaze downwards, to not look on Ella. But he failed. It was as if his eyes were drawn to her face, unable to look elsewhere.

'What do you want me to do?' he asked in a small voice. Jim's heart skipped a beat. This plan might just work!

# 27

Mike, Mason and Jake rode up to the stockyard. The chutes were full, waiting for the next train to come and take the beeves away. 'Howdy, Marshal,' called Linden, one of the men working at the yard. 'How are you today?'

'Good,' Jake replied. 'I got a little business for you. The boss around?'

Linden directed them to Montgomery's office. Montgomery had seen the stockyard boom in the last few years as business had moved from other cow-towns such as Abilene. He had also been in the game long enough to know that the cattle business wasn't a straightforward one. Sometimes it was hard to tell right from wrong. And sometimes it was good for business to believe the town marshal's cock and bull story. Montgomery knew what cattle dealers and cattle rustlers looked like, and the man with Jake Bradman certainly looked and acted like a cattle rustler. He had an obnoxious air of confident arrogance, because of his association with the law in Ellsworth. But it was also because of this association that Montgomery turned a blind eye to the brands on the cattle that were brought into his yard later that evening, driven by Jake, Mike and two other no-good fellers. After all, in a town like Ellsworth, the marshals tended to change faster than the whiskey bottles.

Flush with their cash, Mike, Jake, Mason and Lopez made their way down the street. As they neared the Southern Belle Costello emerged from the shadows by the side of the building.

'Well?' Mike asked.

'No sign of her. If she's in that building she hasn't come out. I've kept a close eye all day.' Costello's heart was racing. He knew that lying to Mike brought with it a possible death sentence but he felt that this was something he had to do. That this was the only way that he could put an end to his association with this gang. The only way to begin his life anew.

'What's the plan, boss?' Lopez, as always, was eager for action.

'It's early yet,' Mike replied. 'Let's go for a drink first, celebrate our success.' They all looked at him in surprise for a moment but then started making their way towards the door of the saloon, none of them willing to turn down the offer of a drink.

'Not you boys,' Mike said to Costello and Lopez. 'I've got something I want you both to do.' Costello's blood ran cold. He knew Jim and Ella hadn't prepared for whatever stunt Mike was about to pull. Mike called Costello and Lopez to him and explained his plan.

Rose was behind the bar with her father when she saw Mike, Jake and Mason walk in. She tried hard to hide the look of both surprise and fear that crossed her face. She hadn't told her father of what she, Jim and Ella had planned, afraid that he would insist on involving himself in something that might cost him his life. She looked across at him. He, too, had noticed the three men entering his saloon. His face remained neutral, his expression unreadable. But Rose could tell by the vigorous way he dried the glass in his hand that he was on edge. These customers were not welcome.

She thought about darting out back to warn Jim, but Mike had fixed his eyes on her and was headed in her direction.

She couldn't move without attracting suspicion and the last thing she wanted to do was to spark a gunfight in the Southern Belle.

'Well hello Rose.' Mike's leering grin creased his features. He looked like a hungry dog, Rose thought.

'Howdy,' she grunted in reply, not even pretending to be civil with him. This was a man who both disgusted and frightened her. Ella's words rang in her ears: *He intends to replace me with you.* She could see the proprietorial gleam in his eyes, in his bearing. She could sense the aggressive superiority emanating from his very being. You will soon be mine, he was thinking. *To do with what I like.*

'Three whiskeys, beautiful.' Rose poured the drinks quickly without saying a word. As she withdrew the bottle she felt a hand on her lower arm. It was Mike's, his sweaty palm making her skin crawl. 'How's about you join us for a drink yourself? Be sociable, like.' Mike's grip on her arm tightened, she thought of yelling out, of calling to her father but she thought better of it. They held all the aces. Looking into Mike's eyes, she wondered whether he knew. Wondered whether he was aware that he was being betrayed by Costello. Maybe they had underestimated him. By splitting his men into two groups he held the upper hand. She couldn't be sure that Costello and Lopez weren't approaching the rear of the building where Ella and Jim were hiding. She could only hope that Costello would come through for them.

Her helplessness weighed heavily on her, however. She had to do something. She was not a passive person, not used to bending to someone else's will. Certainly not someone like Mike Bradman.

'Sure, why not?' she said in response to Mike's offer of a drink. She flashed him her most winning smile. In surprise, Mike loosened his grip on her arm and she pulled it free. She slammed a glass on the counter, filled it and drank it down in one.

'Watch out,' Mike shouted. 'This girl's thirsty.' He could barely keep himself under control. Jake just sat beside him, glaring at him. Mason sat apart, watching the room.

Mike downed his whiskey and Jake followed suit. The liquid had burned Rose's throat as it went down. She quickly poured them another, as well as one for herself. She could sense her father looking across at her, wondering what she was playing at. He knew better than to question his daughter's intentions, however, even when it involved those jiggers.

They reached for their glasses, Mike and Jake tilting their heads back and throwing the alcohol down. Now was her chance. She dropped her glass on to the floor, smashing it into pieces.

'Oh!' she exclaimed. Mike and Jake put their glasses back on the counter. 'Sorry fellers,' she said and gave them a sweet smile. 'I'll just get something to clean that up.'

She was gone before they could say a word. She moved fast, bursting through the door that led to the kitchen.

'Jim,' she called as she came in, 'we'd better be careful . . . ' Her words ebbed away. Jim and Ella were sitting at the kitchen table, the guns of Costello and Lopez trained on them. She turned to go back to the bar, panic rising in her throat.

'I don't think so, missy.' Mike stood in her way. 'You just get back in there and sit down.'

She called for her father, fear and desperation obvious in her voice. He came into the room, all right, but he had Jake's gun wedged in his back.

'What the hell's going on?' he boomed, taking in the situation that was unfolding before him in his very own kitchen. He glared at Mike. 'I don't know what this is all about, but I can tell you for sure that you fellers better get off my premises or . . .'

'Or what?' Jake sneered. 'You'll call the marshal? As far as I can see, he's already here.' Jake shoved him forward roughly. Rose's father stumbled and hit his head against the kitchen table. He collapsed heavily to the ground. Both Rose and Jim leapt up, her cry filling the room. Jim was immediately hit with the butt of Mike's gun across his cheek. Pain flared across his face as he collapsed back into his chair, his head in his hands.

Rose fell on the prone body of her father and pulled him tight to her. 'Get out!' she roared. 'Get out of our house!'

Tears streamed down her face, from anger almost as much as from concern for her father. Jim's vision cleared and he took the opportunity to act. He could only see out of one eye due to the swelling of his cheek but that was enough. His head felt as if it were about to explode but he focused hard, suppressing the agony. He shoved his chair violently backwards by planting his boots on the floor and pushing with his legs. The wooden back slammed into Mike's knees, causing him to shout out in pain and stagger backwards. Jim sprang to his feet, anxious to take advantage of the commotion. He swung at Jake, his fist crashing satisfyingly into the marshal's nose. Blood sprang from the nose as if from a well, streaming down his face. As Jim turned to take on the others he heard Rose cry out.

'No!' she screamed and he found out why almost instantly. A shot rang out and a fiery pain burned in his shoulder. He slumped to the ground beside Rose and her father, the pain immobilizing him. Slowly, despite Rose's pleading and crying, he slipped into unconsciousness. Just before the black veil descended he heard another shot ring out, the first of many more. He missed the splintering of wood as furniture was shot to pieces. The cries of wounded and dying men filled the room but he did not hear them either. He was out cold, blood seeping from his shoulder.

\* \* \*

Rough hands gripped him. 'Jim, are you all right?'

He moaned, reaching through the darkness towards the voice.

'He's been hit. In the shoulder,' he heard the voice say. 'But at least he's still alive.' He felt himself being picked up off the floor and placed on a chair. He slumped down but the arms still held on to him, holding him in place. He felt something being pressed against his wound and the pain cut through his drowsiness, bringing him round. He shouted through gritted teeth, unable to hold back his discomfort. His eyes opened and he stared into the face of Harry McIntyre.

'You sure got yourself into some trouble now, Jim,' he said softly. 'What happened?'

'Harry, you're up,' Jim exclaimed. He had to bite back the pain.

'No choice,' Harry replied, 'with all the noise that you were making down here.'

Jim couldn't dwell on the happiness he felt at seeing Harry, however. 'Rose,' he whispered hoarsely. 'Where's Rose?'

Harry was quiet. Alarm surged through Jim's body, jolting him upright. 'I said, where's Rose?'

'I don't know, Jim,' Harry replied. 'This place is a mess. Its like a slaughterhouse. I don't know . . . ' His voice trailed off. Jim forced himself to his feet and took in the destruction around him.

Three men lay sprawled on the floor, blood pooled around their bodies.

Rose's father was nowhere to be seen and, more worryingly, neither was Rose. But there seemed to be another body, underneath a figure that he recognized as Costello. A foot poked out from underneath his prone body. What chilled Jim to the bone, however, was not the presence of another dead body, but the fact that the foot was unmistakably female. Jim struggled to cross the floor to where the bodies lay.

'Please, no. Not Rose.' His breath shortened, his nerves frayed. He bent down slowly to Costello's body. He grabbed him by the jacket and pulled him over. The pain in his shoulder was hardly bearable. Costello turned over and thumped on to the ground on his back. Jim had to force himself to look at the body that had lain underneath him. He drew in his breath sharply and had to put his hand out against the wall to steady himself. It was Ella.

'They took her.' Jim barely heard the words being spoken, so weak was the voice. 'They took Rose.' A chill ran through his body. He looked down at the source of the voice, the mangled form of Costello. 'Mike, Jake and Lopez. I managed to get Mason but they still shot Ella. They shot her, Jim.' Costello looked at Ella, her hair matted with blood. 'They shot her.' His voice was barely a whisper.

'I'm sorry, Costello. I really am.' Jim whispered.

Harry gripped Jim's shoulder gently. 'They can't be gone far,' he said. 'I saw the jiggers riding out of town when I came downstairs. If we leave now we might catch them, at least see their trail.'

Jim placed his hand on Costello's shoulder. He could feel Costello's life draining away and as he turned to leave he knew he was leaving behind a dead man. As he was about to leave the saloon, Rose's father appeared from one of the bedrooms, a large bump on his head.

'Get her back, Jim,' he said. 'Just get her back.' Jim just nodded his head and dashed out the door. Harry followed close behind just stopping for a moment to pick something up off the floor. He knew instantly what it was, Jim's leather pouch. It must have been shot off by the bullet that caught him in the shoulder. Jim was too far ahead now to call him back and give it to him. He put it in his pocket until later.

Jim clambered on to Jesse's back, ignoring the pain in his shoulder.

'Let's go, boy,' he whispered. 'As fast as you can.' Harry brought his mount alongside. 'No, Harry,' Jim said, 'you're not able.'

Harry just glared across at Jim. 'You were there when I needed you. Now it's my turn.' They rode off hard out of town, Harry doing his best to ignore the searing pain in his ribs.

The moon was high in the sky, providing them with some guidance as they rode. Jesse's flanks were frothy with sweat but still Jim didn't give him any respite. Not that he looked for any. They reached the fork in the road but

Jim didn't stop and turned for the Baker homestead. Harry didn't question his partner, it was as if some inner drive was forcing him on. Calling him to Rose.

*Nearly there*, Jim thought.

He fought to control his thoughts, to formulate a plan, but failed to do so. He was being driven onwards by one impulse only: to rescue Rose. If they had left for Kansas City he knew that he might never catch them. He urged Jesse on once more. He had to get her back.

\* \* \*

'Damn that Costello!' Mike barked, 'I never liked him. Should never have trusted him.' Jake sat silently in the corner of the kitchen, brooding.

'It's all Ella's fault,' he said at last. 'You should have killed her when you had the chance.'

Mike just nodded. He looked over at Rose, slumped against the wall of the kitchen, her legs and wrists bound with rope. She stared back defiantly.

'When Jim comes you fellers are going to wish you had never set foot in Ellsworth,' she hissed.

'I don't think your Jim is going anywhere,' Jake replied, 'except to meet his maker. Last I saw he was shot.' He leered at her and reached out a hand to caress her face. She turned her head away sharply and the two brothers laughed.

He was right, of course. Jim had been shot. Rose knew that. But deep down inside she couldn't believe that he was dead. When the bullets started flying she had seen him fall beside her but he had definitely still been breathing. She remembered Costello opening fire on Lopez and then on Mason, but Mike and Jake had responded by hitting both Ella and Costello himself. It was then that the gunfire had ceased and Mike had ripped her away from her father and brought her back here. What they planned to do next she did not know, but she knew that she had to cling to some hope of rescue. Some hope that her beloved Jim was still alive.

'We had it good here, too, brother,' Jake said wistfully. 'At least I had until you came along.' Although he said it as a joke, there was a barb to his words. Mike just ignored him. 'Marshal. Able to do what I wanted when I wanted. Able to get any woman I liked.' Here, he looked at Rose once more and placed a kiss on her cheek. She recoiled violently.

'Hey, take it easy!' Mike barked. 'She's mine, remember?'

'Sure, I remember,' Jake replied darkly. 'Everything is yours.' He stood and glowered at his brother, real menace in his voice. Mike was taken aback by this sudden mood of aggression. He was taken by surprise, at a disadvantage as he stared up at Jake.

'When we get to Kansas, I'll make it up to you, all right?'

'Brother,' Jake whispered, 'we ain't going to Kansas.' He had his Colt raised and aimed before Mike could even comprehend what was happening. A single shot rang out and Mike lay dead in his chair.

Jim and Harry heard the shot, followed by a woman's scream. They were just about a quarter of a mile away now and the noise was easily heard in the still night air.

'No,' Jim whispered. 'I can't be too late.' Frantic, now, he plunged onwards, any thought of scheming or planning gone from his head. They passed through the copse where Jim had found Ella, and went on down the hill towards the house. A light was visible in a window.

'Please be here,' he mumbled, willing it to be so. He jumped off Jesse's back, not even waiting for him to stop. Harry followed just moments later. The landing jolted Jim's shoulder but he ignored the stab of pain and pulled his Colt from his holster. He kicked the front door in and burst into the kitchen where he was met by the sight of Mike's bloody body. He didn't have time to delight in the fact that it wasn't Rose's body he was staring at, however, as he heard the click of the hammer of a revolver behind him.

'Drop the gun, Deputy.' Jim began to turn but the voice barked out again, viciously. 'I said, drop the gun, Jim. Or else she gets it.' Jim heard a muffled cry from behind him. This time he did drop his gun and turn slowly round, his hands out from his sides to show that he was unarmed. Harry was about to cross the threshold of the house when the menacing voice stopped him in his tracks. He backed away slowly, holding his breath. He was unseen.

Standing before Jim was Jake, his revolver in one hand, the bound figure of Rose enveloped by his other arm. Jim stared into her eyes. Sheer, unadulterated fear stared back at him.

'Let her go, Jake,' Jim said, keeping his voice as even as possible. 'She's done nobody any harm.'

'I don't think so,' Jake replied. He

leered menacingly at Jim. 'You don't remember me, do you?'

Jim was confused. 'What do you mean? Of course I remember you, Jake.'

'That's not what I meant, little Jimmy. Tom's son.'

Jim froze, as if a winter breeze had crept through the open door and down his back. 'What are you saying?' Jim whispered quietly. 'Have we met before?'

Jake just laughed. 'You know we have. The name Burton mean anything to you? When you walked into my office I thought you had come to kill me. I couldn't believe you didn't recognize me. But then I suppose this . . . ' he used the tip of his gun to point out his scar and eye-patch, 'makes me look a little different. How long has it been?' he continued. ' '68 wasn't it? When your father got stamped all over?'

Jim was shaking, a mixture of anger, fear and the strain from all the memories he had banished long ago overwhelming him. He had tried to erase all memories of that fateful night, and the leering, furious figure of Burton standing over him had been banished by the years of drinking.

'I gave him the coffee that night, but of course he gave it to his poor, cold, weak son. It was never meant for you. The coffee was spiked. He was supposed to fall asleep, we keep you quiet and we take the cattle. Simple as that. But you ruined everything. There was no need for anyone to get hurt. But then you fell off your horse. And you know the rest.'

Jim could barely stand. He felt as if he had been hit by a train. 'The coffee was spiked?' he said, his voice barely a whisper. 'It wasn't my fault I fell asleep on watch?'

'Makes no difference, your father's still dead.'

'But I didn't fall asleep!' Jim's voice was more forceful.

'No, but — '

Jim cut him off in mid sentence. 'You killed him. It wasn't my fault.'

Jake was taken by surprise by the fury

in Jim's voice. He had thought he had him broken, but obviously not.

'Well, you'll be joining him soon, anyway. You can discuss it then.'

Jim glared at him. The revelation had lifted a weight from his conscience, but it had also served to intensify his hatred for the man opposite: the man holding a gun to the head of the love of his life.

'Let her go,' Jim spat.

'I don't think so, Jim. The way I see it, she might just want to stay with me, now.'

Jim's face showed his confusion. 'Give her to me and I'll let you go. Forget that you were ever here in Ellsworth.'

'That's not the way it's going to work, I'm afraid, Jim. The way I see it, everyone who knows about me is dead, except you, Rose and her father. So if I kill you, that will only leave Rose and her father. And I'm sure Rose will grow to love me, won't you . . . ' Here, he looked into her terrified face and stroked her nose with his hand, ' . . . if I agree to let your father live in exchange for your hand in marriage?'

Jake's madness went even deeper than Mike had suspected. He thought that he could go back to being marshal of Ellsworth and marry Rose despite all the blood on his hands. Jim felt the situation slipping away from him, felt that he was losing control and running out of ideas. His shoulder throbbed with pain, making him feel weak. The only thing that kept him going was the terrified woman upon whom Jake had such a tight grip.

Harry had listened in amazement and shock to Jake's revelations. He steeled himself, waiting for the right time to enter the house. He readied his revolver, took a deep breath and braced himself to launch himself through the door. The feel of cold steel against his temple stopped him dead.

'I don't think so,' hissed Lopez. Harry dropped his gun and allowed himself to be guided in through the open door by Lopez.

Hope jolted Jim when he saw Harry

enter only for it to be crushed when he saw Lopez's gun pressed against his friend's head. Harry gave Jim a rueful look, sorrow in his eyes. He had tried his best but had failed his friend when it mattered most.

'Lopez!' Jake sounded surprised. 'I thought you'd run off.'

'No, Jake,' Lopez replied, a steely edge to his voice. He looked at Mike's lifeless body, sprawled on the ground. 'What happened to the boss?' he asked, trying hard to keep his voice neutral.

'We had a disagreement,' Jake answered. His hand moved so fast that Jim wasn't even sure he had seen it happen. Two shots rang out and Lopez slumped to the ground with bullets through his head and chest. He was dead within seconds.

Jim dived for his gun on the ground but Jake was faster than him, squeezing off a shot just as Jim laid hands on his weapon. The bullet splintered the floor by Jim's hand, causing the sharp wood to cut his arm but he kept moving, as if the pain didn't even register. He rolled to his right towards the kitchen table and yanked at its legs. The table toppled over on its side and Jim cowered behind its top, which now afforded some cover. Harry reached down, grabbed Lopez's gun and retreated through the door.

'Let her go, Jake,' Jim roared, his voice frayed with emotion. Jake looked frantically around the room. He had his gun jammed so hard into Rose's neck that she was finding it hard to breathe.

'I'll kill her,' he shouted maniacally. 'I'll kill her.' His voice was frayed, panicked. This wasn't going as he'd hoped. 'Show yourself, Jim. Show yourself or she dies.'

Jim could hear Rose's sharp breaths as she struggled to breathe. Who knew what Jake might do?

'Hold on, Jake,' Jim called. 'I'm coming out, take it easy.' Jim stood up slowly, showing that he was unarmed.

'And your friend, too.'

'Do it, Harry,' Jim called. Harry came through the door carefully. He held his revolver up and emptied the bullets on to the ground.

'Your gunbelt, too.'

Harry slipped the belt off. He was now totally unarmed. Jake chuckled. Jim could see no way out. All he could do now was to plead for Jake to have mercy on Rose. It was breaking his heart, to be so close to the one he loved only to have her taken from him. And, worse, to go to a man like Jake. But at least she would be alive, and maybe in the future she would find some way to be free.

'Kill me, then. Just let her live.' Jim looked one last time at Rose; her face was contorted in anguish. He closed his eyes and dropped his head, he would never see Rose again. Harry watched Jake raise his revolver, all his attention now on Jim. Harry reached into his pocket with his left hand while opening the cylinder and sliding in the bullet from the pouch.

'Much obliged,' Jake muttered to Jim as his finger tightened on the trigger and a deafening noise filled the room.

Jim opened his eyes. He was still breathing. Across from him both Jake and Rose lay on the floor, blood pooling around them. He dashed across, unable even to begin to comprehend how he was still alive. He grabbed Rose's body and shook her. No response. He lifted her up. Blood smeared one side of her face. He wiped it with his hand but could find no wound. He shook her again, his raw cry ringing out.

'Rose!'

A quiver of an eyelid was followed by a low moan. She was alive, he barely dared to believe it. Her eyes opened and she stared into Jim's face.

'Are you hurt?' he asked softly. She just shook her head, the blood wasn't hers. He held her to him, vowing never to let her go. He wasn't even aware of the other figure in the room. Standing at the doorway was Harry McIntyre, his smoking revolver in his hand after firing Tom Boland's bullet into Bradman's head.

# 28

**Two months later**

Another hard day's work completed, Jim slumped into his chair at the kitchen table. He took off his hat and gunbelt and hung them over the back of the chair.

'How was work?' asked the voice from behind him.

'Long and tiring,' Jim replied. 'This is one tough town.'

He felt the soft touch of her arms on his shoulders. They reached down the front of his shirt and fingered the shining badge that hung on it. 'That's why they made you the marshal,' she replied.

Jim looked up into her soft blue eyes and caressed her red, curly hair.

'I couldn't do it without you, Rose,' he muttered contentedly, 'my beautiful wife.'